A NON-BLONDE CHEERLEADER
in Love

BOOKS BY KIERAN SCOTT

I Was a Non-Blonde Cheerleader

Brunettes Strike Back

A Non-Blonde Cheerleader in Love

A NON-BLONDE CHEERLEADER
in Love

KIERAN SCOTT

G. P. PUTNAM'S SONS

Special thanks to my All Star cheer squad:
Sarah Burnes, Jen Bonnell, Wendy Stewart, Shira Citron and
Ally Stevenson, all of whom always make me feel like I can do no wrong.
(You guys can fight over who gets to be captain.)

As always, I'd also like to thank my family, Mom, Erin and Ian,
for their encouragement, support and, well, their plain old silliness.

To my myspace cheerleading friends and all the fans who have written
to me, thanks for keeping me in the know and inspiring me every day.
As long as there are girls as fabulous, intelligent and positive as you
out there, I know there's a reason to keep on working!

Most of all, thank you to Matt, who just keeps making me happy.

G. P. PUTNAM'S SONS
A division of Penguin Young Readers Group. Published by The Penguin Group.
Penguin Group (USA) Inc., 375 Hudson Street, New York, NY 10014, U.S.A.
Penguin Group (Canada), 90 Eglinton Avenue East, Suite 700, Toronto, Ontario, Canada M4P 2Y3
(a division of Pearson Penguin Canada Inc.).
Penguin Books Ltd, 80 Strand, London WC2R 0RL, England.
Penguin Ireland, 25 St. Stephen's Green, Dublin 2, Ireland (a division of Penguin Books Ltd.).
Penguin Group (Australia), 250 Camberwell Road, Camberwell, Victoria 3124, Australia
(a division of Pearson Australia Group Pty Ltd).
Penguin Books India Pvt Ltd, 11 Community Centre, Panchsheel Park, New Delhi - 110 017, India.
Penguin Group (NZ), Cnr Airborne and Rosedale Roads, Albany, Auckland 1310, New Zealand
(a division of Pearson New Zealand Ltd).
Penguin Books (South Africa) (Pty) Ltd, 24 Sturdee Avenue, Rosebank, Johannesburg 2196, South Africa.
Penguin Books Ltd, Registered Offices: 80 Strand, London WC2R 0RL, England.

Published simultaneously in Canada. Printed in the United States of America. Design by Marikka Tamura.
Text set in Garth Graphic.
Library of Congress Cataloging-in-Publication Data
Scott, Kieran, 1974–   A non-blonde cheerleader in love / Kieran Scott.   p. cm.
Summary: When the Sand Dune High cheerleading squad goes coed, Annisa and the rest of the team must
learn to get along without turning the season into a battle of the sexes. [1. Cheerleading—Fiction.
2. Interpersonal relations—Fiction. 3. High schools—Fiction. 4. Schools—Fiction.] I. Title.
PZ7.S42643Boy 2007   [Fic]—dc22   2006014268   ISBN 978-0-399-24494-0
1 3 5 7 9 10 8 6 4 2
First Impression

For Peyton, MacKinley, Ava, Ryan, Dylan and Amanda

"He's coming, everyone!" Tara Timothy hissed with one of her patented no-nonsense glares. "Get ready!"

The dozens of students and faculty members that had gathered in the lobby for the impromptu wrestling pep rally instantly fell silent. No one messed with Tara Timothy, fear-inspiring leader of the Sand Dune High cheerleading squad. Excuse me, the *national champion* Sand Dune High cheerleading squad. We had just won at nationals a few weeks back and I still liked the ring to our nifty little title. Sometimes I still couldn't believe that I, Annisa Gobrowski, former member of a fairly uninspired cheer squad from New Jersey, was now a member of the greatest squad in the land.

I stood on my tiptoes to see through the glass doors of the school. Sure enough, K. C. Lawrence's blue Jeep Wrangler had just pulled into a space near the top of the parking lot.

Together with the rest of the squad, I backed up under the light-blue-and-yellow "Pin 'Em Crabs!" banner we had all worked on at Tara's house the night before. Suddenly I felt someone's arms encircling my waist from behind.

"Hey, Jersey," Daniel Healy whispered in my ear.

My heart fluttered around in my chest as his warm breath made goose bumps pop out all over my skin.

1

"Hey, yourself," I replied over my shoulder, feeling oh so cutesy coupley.

Daniel, blond, tan and *huhmana-huhmana* as ever, quickly smooched my cheek. Yes, *my* cheek. He was my very own hunk of boyfriendly perfection. Mine all mine. Daniel was my very first boyfriend and, even better, this was going to be my very first Christmas *with* a boyfriend. That's right, the holiday to end all holidays was just around the corner and with Daniel in my life I had *so* much to look forward to. Kisses under the mistletoe, long walks in the snow . . . I mean, the sand . . . Ah, it was going to be perfection. When I had moved to Florida from New Jersey a couple months back, I had thought my life was pretty much over. But lately things were seriously looking up.

Daniel gave me a squeeze and whispered in my ear again. "I missed you."

"You walked me to school ten minutes ago," I told him, blushing.

"Longest ten minutes of my life," he replied.

"Ugh. Could you guys be any more dramatic?" Sage Barnard said, flipping her Jessica Simpson curls over her shoulder. "Spare us."

Sage shot us an irritated scowl—as she always did whenever Daniel touched, kissed or even breathed the same air as me—then moved to the other end of the squad line. I didn't know what her problem was. She and Daniel had been broken up for a couple of months now and she already had a new boyfriend. His older brother Christopher.

I know. Ick.

"So, how does it feel to be a civilian?" I asked Daniel.

2

"And to not be wearing a tie?" he said with a grin. "Darn good."

Daniel was not in a shirt and tie like the rest of the wrestling team because he had recently quit so he could concentrate on his music—guitar, to be exact. I was still proud of him for standing up to his father and Christopher—who was a senior and still on the team. Until this year both Daniel and Christopher had played football in the fall, wrestled in the winter and run track in the spring. They were so alike that Christopher's friends took to calling Daniel "Mini-Chris." But now that Daniel had found his own thing, they'd have to come up with a new nickname.

"Here he is! Healy, back off!" Tara demanded, thrusting one of her poms at him.

Daniel instantly released me and took a few steps back, hands raised.

Moments later the glass door swung open and K. C. Lawrence, superstar of the SDH wrestling team, walked in. K.C. was on the short side (good wrestlers often are, I'm told—something to do with center of gravity), but totally buff. He was perpetually tan, as most of the kids around here were, and you could see the green of his eyes from about a mile away. He also had long, blond surfer hair that just grazed his shoulders.

No wonder half the girls in school seemed so ready to swoon at the sound of his name. He was definitely drool-inspiring.

"Let's hear it for K.C.! Junior Olympic champion!" Tara shouted.

K.C. stopped in his tracks, trapped in the metaphorical

spotlight. He clutched the strap on his backpack and stared at us all, stunned.

"K.C.! K.C.! K.C.!" everyone chanted, clapping to the beat.

Finally K.C. ducked his head, waved, blushed and smiled. Then Tara beckoned him over. "Speech!" she shouted. "Everyone wants to hear how you're going to lead the wrestling team to states this year!"

Cheers everywhere. K.C. looked like he'd rather do anything but address the crowd, and my heart went out to him. Some people were just not down with public speaking. (Myself not included. But I guess that's obvious or I wouldn't be a cheerleader, choir member and spring musical hopeful.) Still, it seemed like a better idea to do what the masses wanted than to contradict dozens of shouting teenagers hopped up on Starbucks and sugar cereal. Eventually he walked forward and stood next to Tara. The crowd was rapt.

"Uh . . . how am I going to lead the wrestling team to states this year?" he said, looking around. We waited anxiously. "Uh . . . I guess we'll just win."

He shrugged and everyone cracked up laughing, cheering some more. His teammates loved it and clapped louder than anyone.

The crowd started to disperse as the wrestling team practically carried K.C. out of the room. Daniel went along with them, all caught up in the testosterone of the moment, I'm sure. Tara looked at her friend and our teammate Phoebe Cook and her shoulders slumped.

"Well. That was worth all the effort," she said sarcastically.

Just then, my best friend Bethany Goow loped through the front doors, her eyes hidden behind her dark sunglasses, her hair freshly dyed a psychedelic shade of red for the holidays. She looked around at the pom strings on the ground and the banner above.

"What'd I miss?" she asked, yanking the earbuds out of her ears. I could hear the loud wail of electric guitar from ten feet away.

"Nothing you would've wanted to be a part of," I told her as we walked toward the front hall and our lockers.

"What?" she shouted.

"I *said,* 'Nothing you'd want to be a part of!'" I replied. "You're going deaf with that thing, you know."

"Thanks, Mom. I'll take that into consideration," Bethany told me, reaching into her bag to shut off her iPod.

"Hey, guys!" Mindy McMahon, another friend and member of the football cheerleading squad, fell into step with us.

"Barbie," Bethany greeted her with a nod.

"Elmo," Mindy shot back.

Bethany smirked. "Touché," she said. "Someone's learning."

Mindy shook her head, but I could tell she was proud of herself. It wasn't every day Mindy was able to come up with a comeback and I was glad that she had. If she had tried to argue the similarities between her physical self and the most famous doll in the universe, Bethany would have definitely won the debate. Tall, naturally beautiful and healthfully tan, Mindy wore a light pink sundress with a blue sweater over it, looking like she'd just stepped out of a 1950s commercial for clothing detergent.

"I kind of feel bad for K.C.," Mindy said, twirling her

blonde hair tightly around her index finger until the tip turned red. "I mean, all that pressure. Everyone counting on you to go undefeated? I don't think I could handle it."

"That's what that was all about? K. C. Lawrence?" Bethany said, incredulous. "I can't believe I missed it."

Mindy and I exchanged a confused look. "Are you going all school spirit on us now?" I asked.

"Hardly. But even I can get behind a sport in which hot guys in onesies toss each other around on the floor," Bethany said as she unwrapped a fresh Blow Pop. "It's both sexual *and* ridiculous. That's entertainment."

Bethany shoved her lollipop in her mouth and grinned. Mindy paused to study her.

"You know, just when I think you might be semi-normal, you go and say something that totally freaks me out," Mindy said matter-of-factly.

"Intriguing that way, aren't I?" Bethany replied, picking at a scab on her forearm.

Mindy kept walking. "So, Annisa, are you ready for cheerleading tryouts?"

"I think so. Should be interesting," I replied.

"Tryouts! Didn't you just try out? I gotta go through that again?" Bethany whined.

"I'm not trying out," I told her. "We need to find three new girls to replace Mindy, Whitney and Erin for basketball season."

"Yeah. We can't cheer *and* play," Mindy said.

"No. 'Cause that would be, like, hard," Bethany said in a Valley girl voice.

We ignored her. Sometimes that's the only way we can carry out a normal conversation with Bethany around. I loved the girl, but she had this whole "I don't know when to quit" problem. Especially around Mindy. The two of them had been getting along lately for my benefit, I think, but sometimes Bethany just could not stop herself from picking on Mindy, her polar opposite. Luckily Mindy had proven more than capable of letting the jabs glance off her shoulders.

"Who do you think's gonna try out?" Mindy asked me.

"I don't know. But I hope some of the girls from last time come back," I said. "A few of them were pretty good."

"Can we please talk about something else?" Bethany interjected. "Anything else other than cheerleading?"

"Yeah! Like that girl Shira," Mindy said. "She could definitely make it."

"And I'll need a new base with you gone," I said. "She would be great."

"You guys," Bethany said, desperate.

"I almost feel bad for whoever makes it, though," Mindy said. "I mean, the whole Tara Timothy breaking-you-in process?"

We both shuddered. That had not been fun. For anyone.

"I know! I know! *I'll* try out!" Bethany announced, jumping in front of us and throwing her arms up. Actually, girl had a pretty solid high V going. "I can be a base! Here! I'll throw you right now!"

And something told me she would do it too.

"Bethany—"

Mindy and I both stopped in our tracks. At the exact same moment we had seen a colorful flyer on the wall behind Bethany. A flyer that took the breath right out of me.

"Ha! I *knew* that would get your attention!" Bethany

cheered, taking the lollipop out of her mouth and pointing at us with it. "Like I would ever join the lemming brigade. Ha!"

Mindy and I looked at each other, then looked at the flyer again. Finally Bethany seemed to realize that our eyes were not on her.

"What?" she said, and turned around. I watched the glee slowly register on her face as she read. "Guys? They're letting *guys* try out for *cheerleading*? Oh, I *love* this school!" Her ensuing laughing fit could have woken the dead.

"This is very not good," Mindy said.

The sign read, "Tryouts for the basketball cheerleading squad this Friday. All interested girls and BOYS are invited to try out! Informational meeting today at 3:00 P.M. Lecture Hall #210."

Talk about a holiday surprise. Had Coach Holmes already ODed on eggnog?

"Why didn't Coach warn us about this?" I wondered.

"This is going to change everything," Mindy said.

I wasn't sure whether to laugh or barf. "It . . . *could* be fun . . . ," I attempted. After all, with guys on the squad we could do all kinds of new stunts. Huge pyramids, jaw-dropping tosses. It might be exactly what we needed to take our game up a notch.

"Oh, come on, guys! Be serious," Bethany said. "No male in this school is ever going to show up for that meeting."

"What makes you so sure?" I asked.

"These gutless wonders?" Bethany said, spreading her arms wide as if to encompass the whole school. "Please. If any of the guys in this place showed even one iota of originality, there would be mass hysteria. We're talking rain of toads. Cats with nine tails. Babies born with inside-out eye-balls. The whole nine."

"Nice imagery," I said.

"Trust me. You have nothing to worry about."

Down the hall there was a burst of laughter. Bethany's older brother Bobby—whom I fondly called Lumberjack Bob because of his massive size and impressively dark stubble—was strutting around in a little circle, wagging his hips and flailing his arms comically while chanting "SDH! SDH!" in a high-pitched voice. His friends were practically rolling on the floor with laughter. Like this was such an inspired and original performance.

Yeah. A guy trying out for the cheerleading squad would pretty much be signing himself up for endless public mockery. That much was clear.

"I rest my case," Bethany said. "Your precious squad is gonna be fine."

"I think it's going to be so cool having guys on the squad," Lindsey Ryan said that afternoon.

"As long as they're the *right* guys," Sage put in.

Good old Sage. Always reminding us there were right people and wrong people. What would we ever do without her? Tumble into complete and total social oblivion, I suppose.

It was five minutes after three and the entire squad—minus Mindy, Whitney and Erin—had gathered in front of the blackboard in lecture hall #210. We were supposed to be lined up in height order, but instead we were huddled into a clump, speculating about this whole guys-on-the-squad thing. So far, of the twelve or so cheerleading hopefuls seated in the room, not one of them was sporting a Y chromosome. It looked like Bethany was right. The guys of SDH were just not ready to take on cheerleading.

"Please. If a single guy has the guts to walk into this room, I'll pay each of you a million dollars," Chandra Albohm said in her gravelly voice, checking her newly dyed brown hair for split ends. Up until nationals I had been the only non-blonde on the squad—yes, Sand Dune High is the Official Land of the Blondes (we're thinking about having bumper stickers made up)—but then Chandra had decided to dye her stressed strands back to their natural color. And believe me, two was *definitely* company.

"I think you're going to be surprised," Autumn Ross protested. "There are a few enlightened males in this school."

"Oh yeah? Name one," Chandra demanded.

Autumn stared back at her blankly and a slight crinkle formed between her two white-blonde eyebrows. Autumn was very into New Age stuff like meditating and crystals and aromatherapy and chakras, but she wasn't yet all-knowing. Although I think she was working on it in her spare time. Still, she couldn't seem to come up with an answer.

"Yeah. Didn't think so," Chandra said.

"I'll think of one! You know I don't like being put on the spot!" Autumn said, pouting her lips.

"I just can't believe she would do this without telling us," Phoebe said. "This is our squad. Don't we get to have an opinion?"

"Apparently not," Tara said flatly.

Her expression was even more pinched than usual. Everyone had assumed she, as captain, had known about the change, but she had already confessed that she was as clue-less as the rest of us—something that clearly caused her great pain to admit. By not trusting Tara with her plans, Coach had lumped her in with the rest of us lowly minions, and Tara *loved* to be above us all. I think she lived for it, actually.

"I mean, honestly. It's like we don't even matter!" Phoebe ranted, raising her voice a bit. "Just because we're still in high school, that doesn't mean we're not people with feelings and thoughts and, you know, *feelings*!"

"You said that already," Felice pointed out helpfully.

"Well, that's 'cause it's true!" Phoebe snapped.

I glanced at Chandra, disturbed. What was up with Angry Phoebe? I'd met Depressed Phoebe and Mopey Phoebe, but this new mood swing was out of the blue. Clearly this cheer-boys thing had really gotten under her skin.

"Okay, honey, unclench," Tara said, patting her on the back. "I'm thinking no more coffee for you."

Phoebe took a deep breath and rolled her shoulders back, clearly trying to relax. Then the door opened and slammed and Coach Holmes stood there with one eyebrow raised. With her dark skin, dyed blonde ponytail and white track suit, Coach could have been a Beyoncé decoy, especially with the diva-esque attitude she had on just then.

"I believe there was supposed to be some order here, ladies?" she said.

Immediately everyone scurried into place in a straight line, backs to the blackboard. But not before a few brave people, myself not included, shot Coach Holmes betrayed glares. Coach pretended not to notice and hummed to herself as she pulled out her clipboard and pens. It was way too obvious she was trying to avoid eye contact with us. I'd never heard the woman hum before in my life.

Plus, the tune sounded vaguely like, "These Boots Are Made for Walkin'." Very "don't mess with me or I'll kick your butts." Message received, Coach.

Finally, Coach Holmes finished organizing herself and looked up at the small crowd gathered in the seats. I saw her face fall slightly when she realized there were no guys present. Apparently she had overestimated the male population of our little school.

"Looks like her evil plan didn't quite work out the way she hoped," Chandra said in my ear.

"All right! Let's get this meeting started!" Coach announced, recovering quickly.

Then the door opened again and everyone fell silent. The distinct sound of boy laughter was followed by the appearance at the door of none other than Daniel Healy. My Daniel Healy. My gorgeous, beautiful, non-wrestling, guitar-playing Daniel Healy. Who was, apparently, very good at keeping a secret.

"You've *got* to be kidding me," Sage said.

My jaw dropped like a stone. Daniel looked at me, smirked and sauntered into the room. Clearly he was enjoying the expression of total stupefaction on my face. But the shock didn't stop there. He was followed by Terrell Truluck, wide receiver extraordinaire; Steven Schwinn, intrepid *Weekly Catch* reporter; and a big, beefy Asian kid who, for some reason, I knew to be named Joe. A few other guys trickled in and together the boy brigade filled up the back row.

Un-be-freakin'-lievable.

I could *feel* the total bafflement of my squad mates and imagined a huge finger dropping down from the sky, flicking Tara over and knocking us all down like a train of dominoes. Meanwhile, Coach Holmes' smile nearly engulfed the room.

"Did you know he was coming?" Sage asked me.

All I could do was squeak.

"Okay. Was that a yes or a no? I don't speak mouse."

"No, all right? I had no idea," I said through my teeth.

Daniel gave me a jaunty wave, loving every minute of this. I tried to lob back a look of death, but just ended up grinning. Daniel on the cheerleading squad? This could be so, *so* cool!

Coach Holmes checked her watch and walked to the front of the desk. "Thank you, everyone, for coming. As you know, each year we lose a few of our fall squad members to various winter sports and those spaces need to be filled. This year we are down three female athletes, but we will be taking five girls total."

This caused a bit of a stir among the hopefuls, who now saw their chances rise exponentially. We all looked at Tara, who stared straight ahead like a statue. Clearly this was another development she hadn't been privy to.

"Two girls will be taken on as alternates in case of injury or other unforeseen circumstance," Coach continued.

My face flushed scarlet. Obviously Coach had decided on this course of action because of what had happened at the beginning of the year. Two cheerleaders had been tossed off the squad for violating the Athlete's Contract—which was the only reason Mindy and I had been given the opportunity to try out back at the beginning of October. Some members of the squad had blamed me for getting the girls booted—long story—and I knew that a few of them still did. Thus, the hot flash.

"We will also be taking between four and eight men this season," Coach continued. "Now, this is just something I've decided to try out," she said, glancing at the squad to silence any oncoming questions or protests. "The squad does not compete during basketball season, so this will give us a chance to decide whether or not the coed thing works for us. If we decide that it does, we will continue on with it in the fall and compete in a new division next year."

"What's this *we* stuff?" Tara loud-whispered.

My breath caught in my throat. Talking back to Coach Holmes was *not* a wise idea. The entire squad froze like we were in front of a firing squad. When Coach has a major meltdown, it's pretty darn scary. Like "produced by Quentin Tarantino" scary. When that vein in her forehead starts throbbing, we know we're in trouble.

"Plus, having men on the squad will be great for all you ladies who hope to cheer in college," Coach Holmes said pointedly. "Squads are looking for girls with coed experience, so this will put you at the top of the proverbial food chain."

Tara flushed slightly and looked at her feet. We all knew she was hoping to cheer in college next year. She had applied only to big sports schools and had visions of herself cheering on the sidelines at a bowl game, getting her mug on national TV. Coach had just said the exact perfect words to clam Tara up.

For now, anyway.

"So, let's have everyone sign in," Coach Holmes said, returning her attention to the room. "And while you do that, I'll talk a little bit about what it takes to be a Sand Dune High School Fighting Crab."

The entire squad blew out a sigh of relief. No meltdown. We were safe—at least for the time being. But I had a feeling that if we did, in fact, take guys on this season, there was going to be some major drama.

And we'd be seeing a lot more of that vein.

• • •

As soon as Daniel and I were out the back door of the school, I pulled him to me and placed the back of my hand

15

on his forehead. Daniel laughed as he almost fell over from the force of my grip.

"Uh, what're you doing?" he asked.

"Nope. No fever," I joked, regarding him with mock concern. "So what is it? Aneurysm? Stroke? Are you seeing spots? Do you taste pennies?"

"Taste pennies?" he asked.

"That's an indication of something. I just don't know what," I told him.

Daniel laughed. "Should I be offended?" he asked, shrugging out of his varsity football jacket. It was rather toasty under the afternoon sun. Toasty in December. Go figure. "I thought you'd be psyched I was trying out."

"I would! I mean, I am!" I stuttered. "I mean, I would've been more so if I had, I don't know, *known* about it!"

I whacked his arm as we started off toward the football field. Every morning and afternoon when we didn't have conflicting clubs or practices, Daniel and I walked to and from school together. It was always a little bit of a letdown walking home alone after cheerleading, but from the looks of things, I wasn't going to have to deal with that much longer. If Daniel wasn't joking about trying out for the squad, of course. And if he was any good.

Would he be any good? I couldn't even imagine Daniel cheering. Suddenly I had an image of him in a miniskirt doing side hurdlers and I had to bite down hard on the inside of my cheek to keep from laughing.

"Sorry," he said sheepishly, not noticing my internal mirth. "I was going to tell you, but Terrell said the look on your face would be too classic. And man, was he right. I thought you were going to faint in there."

"So did I," I replied. I turned around and walked backward up the hill so I could face him. "So what's the deal? Do you really *want* to be a cheerleader?"

Daniel shrugged. "I don't know. Terrell was joking about it during gym and then we sort of ended up daring each other to do it and it wasn't like I could back out of a dare."

I deflated a little. A dare? It took a dare to get him interested in one of the most important things in my life? "So you *don't* really want to do it."

"No! I don't know! It could be cool," Daniel said, his blue eyes sparkling. "The stunts those guys do at the competitions are sick. And since I'm not wrestling, it seems like it would be a good way to make sure I keep working out this winter."

I turned and fell into step with him. "Plus, it'll look killer on your college applications," I pointed out.

"Definitely," Daniel said. "With jazz band and everything, I'm going to come out of this year looking like the most well-rounded guy on the planet."

"What about jazz band?" I asked. "Won't it conflict?"

"Nah. Not too much. We mostly practice during lunch and our concerts are at night," Daniel said. "I already talked to Holmes about it and she's cool with working around whatever. I think she really wants to take guys."

"I *know* she does," I said, rolling my eyes. "The woman was actually humming."

"What does that mean?" Daniel asked, tilting his head.

"No idea. But it means *something*," I replied.

Daniel laughed and shook his head. Unfortunately, I get that a lot. "Anyway, I think it would be cool to be one of the first guys on the SDH cheerleading squad. I could make history."

Aw. He was so cute! And so very naïve. Yeah he would be making history, but being a guy cheerleader wasn't going to be all fun, all the time. If Bobby's performance that morning was any indication of things to come, Daniel would be in for it. Capital I. Capital T.

"Even though you're going to catch more crap than the grill on the front of a Mack truck?" I teased. I didn't want to make such a big deal out of it that he would change his mind, but I did want him to know what he'd be up against. Therefore, the serious comment in the unserious tone.

"Yeah. Even though," he said, brushing it off. Maybe I should have gone for more serious. He paused and turned to face me. A warm breeze blew his hair around in the back as overhead seagulls cawed. Seagulls in December. Once again, go figure. "Plus, there's that added perk," he said.

I smiled at the flirtatious tone in his voice. "What's that?"

He reached out and tugged on the front of my cheerleading vest. I tripped toward him. Tingles all over. "I get to hang out with you more," he said quietly.

Major heart swoop. Boy sure knew how to make a girl's knees buckle. But he still had to pay for not telling me, and he'd just given me the perfect opportunity to collect. I stood on my tiptoes and leaned in like I was going to kiss him. His eyes got all droopy, making it really hard *not* to touch my lips to his, but I controlled myself. Somehow.

"Hate to break it to you, Healy, but I'm not sure you got what it takes," I said cockily. He blinked, and I pushed him backward with both hands before strutting off.

"Hey!" he said, regaining his balance and jogging to catch up with me. "That was supposed to be romantic!"

"You want romantic?" I said, slipping out of my back-pack. "Carry my books."

I handed the two-ton bag over (we had midterms coming up) and kissed him quickly on the lips before sauntering away again.

"Wow! You really don't like to be kept in the dark!" Daniel called after me with a laugh. I turned around, my pleats dancing, and walked backward.

"And don't you forget it!" I said with a smile.

"Relegated to the cafeteria," Chandra muttered as we shoved through the double doors into the large, airy caf, which was bordered by a courtyard full of outdoor tables. The room still smelled of overboiled hot dogs and cardboard pizza, with a slight oniony after-scent. "I mean, how do you win nationals and then get relegated to the cafeteria?"

"The boys' basketball team has the gym, the girls' basketball team has it after them, and the wrestling team has the auxiliary gym," I said. "Thus, the cafeteria."

"Yeah. And what has the boys' basketball team ever done for us?" Chandra said. "Besides sucked all our energy dry, that is."

The SDH basketball team didn't quite measure up to the football and wrestling teams. Like, they weren't even on the same ruler. Last year they had apparently gone 4–12 and been proud of themselves. Not a good sign. But I had experience with cheering for losing teams, thanks to my less-than-stellar school back in Jersey. *Tons* of experience. After dealing with a 0–9 football team, I could cheer for anything. Bring on the losers!

"As far as I'm concerned, this school should be kissing our accomplished butts," Chandra said. She paused in front of the darkened window to the school store and checked her murky reflection, swiping her bangs out of her face with a sigh.

"Sheesh. Tell me how you really feel," I said.

Chandra looked at me and her shoulders relaxed a bit. "Sorry. I haven't had my three o'clock chocolate fix yet."

I reached into my backpack and pulled out the mini bag of M&Ms I hadn't felt like eating after lunch. Chandra's eyes widened as she snatched it from my hands. Girl actually tore the bag open with her teeth.

"Bless you," she said, then dumped half the bag into her mouth at once and closed her eyes, savoring the candy-coated goodness.

"Just try not to choke," I told her, dragging her away from her reflection.

We turned around and paused for a moment to take it all in. All the tables and chairs had been folded and piled up at the far end of the caf, making space for the tumbling mats set up down the center. On the mats a bunch of girls attempted round-off back handsprings one by one, occasionally spazzing and flailing their way to the floor. Two janitors lounged in the corner, one of them leaning on his mop, both watching the proceedings with amusement. They were probably hoping enough people would fall on their butts and slide off the mats so that they'd have less stuff to clean up later.

"It's a travesty," Chandra said.

"You're right. We do deserve a little more R-E-S-P-E-C-T," I said. "But it is only pre-tryout practice."

"All right, people! Let's get our butts in gear and line up

already!" Tara Timothy shouted, slapping her hands together.

"Yeah. Tell that to Tara," Chandra said, rolling her eyes and popping another M&M. She offered me some and I waved her off. She needed it more than I did.

Meanwhile, on the mats, Daniel, Steven, Joe and the other guys—seven of them in all—lined up at the end of the row of girls, looking a little sheepish and out of place. Terrell Truluck, clad in gray sweats and a Sand Dune Football T-shirt, put his hands on his hips and jogged over to Tara prissily, kicking his heels up.

"I'm, like, ready! Okay?" he said in a nasal voice, cocking his head to the side.

A bunch of girls giggled. Tara melted him into a Terrell-shaped puddle with her death-ray glare.

"This is gonna be interesting," I said.

Chandra and I walked over to the wall on the right and sat down next to Autumn, Sage, Lindsey and Jaimee Mulholland, who were already camped out, munching on Baked Lays and watching the drama unfold. Technically, none of us had to be there since we weren't trying out, but who could miss an entertainment opportunity as rare and promising as this one?

"Ten to one Terrell doesn't make it through the first practice," Sage said, crunching into a chip, as we sat.

"I'll take that action," Chandra replied.

Out on the mats, Tara and Terrell were engaged in an old-school face-off. Neither one of them blinked for about two minutes.

"Take a lap," Tara told Terrell finally.

"What?" Terrell barked.

"I don't do laps," Joe piped up behind Terrell. He had a deep voice that reverberated through my bones. I could only imagine the power it would have on the court.

"Then it's a good thing I'm not telling *you* to do one," Tara told him before refocusing her energy on Terrell. "If that's gonna be your attitude, Terrell, you can take a lap."

Terrell blew out a scoff and backed up a few paces. "I ain't takin' no lap."

Apparently he got all gangsta when challenged by authority. Coach Holmes stepped up next to Tara and eyed Terrell with obvious disdain. She had a brand-new whistle with a red strap wrapped around her hand. All the better to keep you in line with, my dear. Under Coach's gaze Terrell finally had the sense to look intimidated. Momentarily, anyway.

"Mr. Truluck, are you disrespecting our captain?" Holmes said, raising her eyebrows.

Terrell's mouth fell open. "I—"

"Because I can't imagine you disrespected your football captain like that," Holmes continued. "I wouldn't even want to *know* what would happen to you if you did."

I held my breath. Terrell looked from Holmes to Tara and back. Then he checked over his shoulder at Daniel, gauging whether or not this dare was worth going through with, I assume. Daniel shrugged. I hoped Terrell wouldn't storm out. Not only because it would be a ridiculously uncomfortable scene, but because there was a chance that if Terrell left, Daniel might bail too. And I had already invested way too much daydream time in visions of Daniel and me on the squad bus together, doing stunts together, smooching behind the bleachers in our uniforms together.

I didn't want to give all that up before I got a chance to actually *do* any of it.

"One lap around the cafeteria?" Terrell said finally.

"Yep," Tara said with a triumphant smirk.

Terrell nodded. "You got it."

Then he sprinted around the caf so fast, you would have thought the mystery meat had sprouted legs, busted free and given chase. He even hurdled right over our outstretched legs, causing Jaimee and Autumn to yelp and squeeze in toward the rest of us. He got back to Tara in 2.5 seconds and wasn't even winded.

"Damn!" I said under my breath.

"He set the state record in the hundred-yard dash last spring," Lindsey said.

"I think he just broke it again," Chandra put in.

Terrell cracked his neck from side to side and put his hands on his hips. "How's that for a lap?"

Tara cleared her throat. "Fine. That was . . . fine."

Terrell laughed and turned toward the line of cheerleading hopefuls, throwing his arms wide, then giving a little bow.

"Aw, yeah!" Daniel said, reaching out his hand for a slap.

Terrell went down the line, smacking hand after hand as his buddies congratulated him, before finally falling in at the end.

"All right, all right, all right!" Coach shouted, quieting the guys down. She walked toward their end of the line and looked them all over. "You know, maybe when I put out the word that I wanted to try a coed squad, I should have specified that I wanted *men*, not boys," she snapped. " 'Cause all I see here is a bunch of immature clowns who wouldn't know their asses from their elbows."

The guys' faces fell serious—even Terrell's.

"Now, are you guys going to take this seriously, or am I going to have to reconsider my decision?" Holmes asked.

Total silence. Daniel looked like he was wishing he was seriously elsewhere. I looked at Tara. From the obvious hope on her face I knew exactly what she was thinking: *Reconsider, reconsider, reconsider . . .*

Apparently she'd decided she would make her college squad on her own, without any help from SDH's male population.

"I *said*, are you guys going to take this seriously?" Coach shouted.

Whoa. There it was. The tendons in her neck strained, joining that throbbing vein in her forehead. Even *my* heart skipped a beat.

"Yes, Coach," Steven Schwinn muttered, then looked at the other guys uncertainly. Steven had seen this routine from Coach before, having covered practices and the national competition for the *Weekly Catch*. He knew how to answer. But clearly the other guys did not.

"*What!?*" Coach shouted.

I seriously thought she might go supernova all over the place.

"Yes, Coach!" the guys said in unison.

"I can't hear you!"

"Yes, Coach!" they all shouted. Joe's voice nearly blew us through the wall. Chandra and I exchanged an impressed glance.

Meanwhile, Coach narrowed her eyes, staring each of the guys down until they looked away, then finally turned and walked by Tara.

"Teach them the cheer," she ordered.

Then I *knew* she was really pissed because she kept right on walking and slammed through the doors. Holmes never missed a minute of pre-tryout practice when I was trying out. She wanted to keep an eye on everyone and assess their progress. If she needed a breather, she was set to pop.

So she would have *definitely* exploded if she had seen what happened next. The second she was gone, the guys all doubled over in laughter.

"This is very not good," I said quietly, echoing Mindy's thoughts upon first hearing about the change.

"Don't worry. Coach will whip them into shape sooner or later," Chandra said confidently.

But as I watched Terrell mimicking Coach's words, Daniel, Joe, and the others struggling for breath, and Tara trying in vain to get their attention, I wasn't quite so sure. Even Steven—who had seen the Wrath of Holmes—was having a hard time controlling himself. He kept working his face into straight submission, then cracking up all over again. As of right now, Coach Holmes was just a big joke to them, and *she* was off somewhere hunting down a punching bag. This whole experiment could be over before it ever got off the ground.

• • •

"What do I get my dad? I never know what to get my dad," Daniel said as we strolled along the pathways of the Beach-front Mall that evening.

The whole place had been built to look like an old-time village with tall torch lights, cobbled walks and palm trees in iron planters. They had gone all out with the Christmas decorations too, stringing fake evergreen garlands, white lights and red bows over the pathways and hanging a wreath on almost every door. Christmas carols were pumped from hidden speakers and fake snow lined some of the buildings. It was quaint, but no matter how much you dressed up a Gap, it was still just a Gap.

Plus, looking at fake snow when it was 75 degrees out was oddly disconcerting.

"I don't know. Maybe a Dolphins jersey?" I suggested.

"He already has, like, ten. Marino, Duper, Williams, Taylor, everyone," Daniel said with a groan. "What do you get your dad?"

"Books. I always get him books," I replied, swinging my little Victoria's Secret bag back and forth. I had picked up a small bottle of my mother's favorite scented moisturizer there while Daniel had waited outside, avoiding looking at the sexy windows with all his might, his face burning brighter than the suit on the rosy-cheeked mall Santa. "We tried getting him a DVD player once, but he almost never used it. Actually, he used it as a base to stack more books."

My father was an English professor at Miami University, and even though it seemed like he had already read every novel and nonfiction tome known to man, he always produced a wish list at least a page long every Christmas, birthday and Father's Day. It made gift buying easier, but also a little bit boring, so I usually gave him something silly too. Like the Hemingway bobblehead that had been stashed under my bed since I had found it back in August at a random gift shop back in Jersey.

"Okay, forget about Dad," Daniel said, pausing in front

of the wishing well, which was now centered by a humongous pile of garishly wrapped fake gifts. "What do *you* want for Christmas?"

Ah, the perfect opener. I loved it when people gave me the perfect opener. It made me feel all smart and stuff.

"I want you to make the cheerleading squad," I said.

Daniel smiled. "Done."

"I'm not so sure about that," I said.

"Is this going to be another knock on my ability? Because I don't think my ego can handle it," he said.

"No. Not at all," I told him. "It's just . . . Coach Holmes takes the cheerleading squad seriously."

"I know," he said.

"*Very* seriously," I added.

"I know." He was getting a little impatient. "I think we all know that after this afternoon."

"So that stuff Terrell pulled today? That was not good," I told him. "And you guys laughing?"

"She didn't even hear that!" Daniel protested.

"Yeah, but Tara did," I told him. "And she is very anti-male."

"Tell that to Bobby Goow," Daniel said with a smirk.

Tara and Bobby had been going out since before puberty set in. How she, with her volatile temper, handled the big doofball, I will never know.

"That's not what I mean," I told him. "She's anti-*you guys*. And if you think she's not going to tell Coach Holmes every single thing you do, then you don't know her as well as I do."

"Girls," Daniel scoffed. Like we were all such huge gossips.

28

"Hey! Don't lump me in with her," I said. "The point is, you guys have to at least *act* like you care about it or Coach is going to pull the plug on the whole thing. Trust me."

Daniel just looked at me with a blank expression that made my stomach turn. He was getting irritated. A couple of little kids ran toward us, then parted around our legs and kept running, headed for Santa's throne. Daniel softened slightly and smiled as he watched them shriek and squeal.

"I'm just trying to help," I told him.

"I know."

"Well . . . *do* you care about making the team?" I asked him tentatively.

"You know I do," he said. "I had fun today."

"Well, then maybe you should tell the other guys to chill a little," I suggested. "Or she won't take guys at all and that'll be that."

Daniel finally nodded and relaxed a little. "Okay," he said. "I'll talk to Terrell. He really wants to be on the squad too, you know. He was just being Terrell. But afterward he kept talking about the stunting video Coach showed us and he's actually pretty psyched."

I smiled. "Good. He'd be fun to have around. If he could, you know, control himself."

Over the past few weeks I'd had plenty of opportunities to hang out with Terrell, thanks to his friendship with Daniel. He was kind of a spotlight hog, but luckily he was also very funny. My stomach always hurt from laughing after we got together. But every once in a while he took his teasing too far. So I figured one of two things was going to happen. Either he'd be good comic relief from Tara, or he'd drive us all insane. I was hoping for the former.

"Don't worry about it. He'll be fine," Daniel said casually as we started walking again. "Hey, so, you know that chair-sit thing? Have you ever done that before?"

His enthusiasm was too cute. "No, actually. I've never done partner stunts before. I guess we're all gonna have to learn new stuff."

Daniel blew out a sigh of relief. "Good. Because it looks like those guys basically grab the girl's butt, you know? And if some guy did that with you—"

"Uh, hello? *You* might be grabbing some *other* girl's butt!" I cried, laughing.

Daniel blanched. So did I. We both stopped walking. My stomach fell so fast, I thought it was going to plop out onto the ground.

"Oh. Right," Daniel said. "Well, I guess if I make the squad, we'll just have to be partners."

I blushed. The very thought sent my pulse racing. "Well, it's all just in the name of sport, right?" I said.

We stared at each other for a long moment. Suddenly all I could think about was him tossing Sage. Looking up at her to keep balance and seeing up her skirt. Her falling and him grabbing her as she came down and his hand landing on her—

"Yeah. We're just gonna have to be partners," we both said at the same time.

Then we turned and got back to the much less stressful activity of Christmas shopping.

• • •

My friends and I stayed away from practices for the rest of the week. If Daniel didn't get through to Terrell, I didn't want to witness another standoff—or know exactly what he

30

was doing—so that I wouldn't hold it against him later. The less I knew, the better. Ignorance was bliss.

But whatever happened in those two days, it apparently hadn't resulted in Coach Holmes having a total mental breakdown or rescinding her decision to go coed, because when Friday evening rolled around, Daniel was waiting out in the gym lobby with the rest of the unnerved hopefuls, getting ready to try out.

And I was sending him good vibes from the center of the bleachers inside the gym. The entire squad had turned out to watch the tryouts and cheer for the newbies. Most of the wrestling and basketball teams—both guys and girls—were there as well. The air was thick with the scents of shampoo and soap since they were all freshly showered after their own practices. The guys' b-ball team had gathered mostly at the tip-top of the stands and were laughing and whispering and generally acting like little kids on a field trip. I knew they were all hyped up to see the guys' auditions. I could practically feel the drip of their saliva on the back of my neck. I just hoped they didn't mock Daniel too hard or I might have to kill them all.

"Hey, Annisa," K. C. Lawrence said, scooting over to sit next to me.

"Hey there, rock star," I said. "How does it feel to be undefeated?"

"It's only been three matches."

"Uh, and three pins," Mindy reminded him, leaning forward so she could see him.

K.C. blushed. "Yeah. Okay. It feels sorta good, actually." He flipped his long hair over his shoulder. "So, you nervous for Daniel?"

"Kind of," I said. "I just hope they don't get on his case or try to mess him up," I added, glancing over my shoulder at Daniel's brother and his friends.

"Don't worry. They say anything, I'll take them down," K.C. said.

"And we all know he's good at it," Mindy put in under her breath.

"Thank you," I said with a smile. "I'm sure Daniel would appreciate that too."

"Yeah, well, I gotta hand it to the dude. He's got guts," K.C. said, looking across the gym. "I'd rather wax my eyebrows off than get out there and do this."

"Now there's an image," I said. Maybe he and Bethany should get together and compare notes.

"Okay, everyone," Coach Holmes called out, standing up next to the judges' table, where five volunteer teachers and guidance counselors sat with their clipboards. Usually Holmes sported trendy track suits or comfy sweats, but today she was wearing jeans and a black turtleneck and her hair was pulled back in a no-nonsense bun. Who knew a hairstyle could be intimidating? She looked up and addressed the crowd. "We're about to get started and we're going to bring in the guys first."

"Whoo-hoo! Bring 'em on!" some loser shouted from the top row, earning cheers and catcalls.

"Hey! Quit it!" K.C. grumbled over his shoulder.

"Thank you, Mr. Lawrence," Coach Holmes said as she leveled the culprit with a glare. "Now I expect you all to treat each and every one of our hopefuls with the respect they deserve," she said firmly. "If any one of you people so much as coughs to cover a laugh, I will kick you out of here so hard, you'll be nursing a tread burn for a week, you got me?"

Silence. Damn, this woman was good.

"All right then," she said.

Coach Holmes turned and walked across the gym, her sneakers squeaking on the shiny wood floor. My heart pounded so fast, it had me looking around for the defibrillator. Thanks a lot, Daniel. I was supposed to be all chill this time around. Instead I felt like I *was* trying out again. Coach swung the door open and we all heard her call out the first name.

"Daniel Healy?"

Oh, God. He was *first*?

Giggles trickled down from above. K.C. shot the guys a derisive glare and shook his head. I was liking this guy more and more by the second. Eventually the door slammed behind Coach and Daniel. The laughter was cut short.

"Are you okay?" Mindy whispered in my ear.

All I could do was nod. My throat was so dry that if I had talked, I might have coughed and then I'd be Coach's first victim. And that whole tread-burn thing did not sound like a good time.

Daniel walked right to the center of the gym, wearing the outfit I had helped him pick out the night before—long SDH Football shorts and a clean white T-shirt. He stood at attention with his hands behind his back, his chest out and his chin up, looking every bit the perfect cheerleader. Someone really *was* taking this seriously.

Daniel smiled at the judges and then his eyes scanned the crowd. When he looked at me, I gave him an encouraging smile and tried really hard not to barf. Barfing might sort of throw him off.

"Okay, Daniel. Whenever you're ready," Coach Holmes said.

Daniel nodded quickly. His feet shifted and he cleared his throat. He was visibly nervous.

You can do it, I thought. *You can, you can, you can!*

"Let's go! Ready? OK!" Daniel shouted in a low voice.

And I almost lost it. A laugh gurgled up in my throat so hard and fast, I almost choked myself trying to hold it back. Mindy grabbed my arm and squeezed and I knew she was two seconds short of a breakdown too. I'd love to say that it was just the nerves—and it was, partially—but it was Daniel too. It was just totally bizarre watching him call a cheer like that. All alone out there in the middle of the court. I mean, he was a *guy*.

Oh my God. Maybe I was sexist!

"S! D! H! S! Let's go, Crabs!" Daniel shouted.

I have no idea how the guys were controlling themselves. Statistically, they really do have a harder time with that than girls do, I think. I glanced at K.C. He was the picture of perfect concentration. Was he trying to send Daniel good vibes too, or was he just focusing really hard on not cracking up?

"S! D! H! S! Let's go, Crabs!" Daniel continued.

"He's pretty good," K.C. said under his breath.

And actually, he was right. Once I really started critiquing Daniel, I realized he had it down. His arms were solid and his clasps were perfect. He even sort of looked like he was having fun. As much as anyone who's that on display can look like they're having fun.

"Sand Dune fans, let's hear you shout!" Daniel cried.

"Let's go, Crabs!" we all cheered along with him.

It was a huge relief to shout. Huge, huge, *huge*.

"Let's go, Crabs!"

"Let's go, CRABS!"

By the end we were screaming. Giddy and screaming and trying really hard not to laugh from the tension and the silliness. Instead we all cheered and clapped and shouted for Daniel. Chandra and K.C. pounded the bleachers with their feet as they applauded and everyone joined in, shaking the whole room.

Even the guys on the top bleacher, who were probably peeing in their pants by this point, cheered like crazy. I hoped that now that they had seen it, they understood that it was not easy to try out, especially not for a guy. Maybe they even respected him a little bit for it. I know I did.

It was a great moment. Daniel stood there calmly as the judges jotted their scores and I was so proud of him. He hadn't messed up the moves once. He'd stayed composed even as the rest of us were totally losing it. He was the first guy ever to try out for the Sand Dune High cheerleading squad and he'd pulled it off. And pulled it off *well*.

I saw Mr. Dumera, the physics teacher, and Mr. Cuccinello, my guidance counselor, exchange an impressed look. An extreme thrill shot right through me. Unless I was mistaken, Daniel and I were about to start seeing a lot more of each other.

"I can't believe how nervous I am," Daniel said as we waited along the gym wall for Coach Holmes to come in and read off the names of the new squad members. He clasped my hand so hard, I swear I heard a couple of bones crack. "I think I'm more nervous now than I was before the tryout."

Wow. So he really did want it. I pulled my hand away and shook it out.

"Ohh. Sorry," he said, biting his lip.

"I'm fine," I told him. "And you made it. I know you did."

"Yeah?" He looked at me as if I actually had some knowledge of the matter. Like my word meant anything. So I'd seen two teacher types smile at each other. So what? Maybe they were sharing a personal joke. Maybe they'd both just eaten really good burritos after school. Maybe they were having an affair. What the heck did I know?

"Yeah," I told him firmly. And hoped I was right.

Daniel looked over his shoulder at Joe, who was lounging back against the wall behind him, staring into space. Now that I'd seen him in a tightish T-shirt, I realized that what I originally perceived as heaviness was actually just serious muscle. Joe was thick all around, but solid thick. Not jiggly thick. As he stood there with his hands behind his back, he flexed one bicep, then the other, then the other.

"You nervous, man?" Daniel asked.

The biceps lay still. Joe looked at Daniel out of the corner of his eye. "I don't do nervous."

Daniel blinked. "Somehow I believe that."

The door squealed open and Coach strode in, clipboard in hand. All the air was sucked right out of the room as everyone held their breath. Daniel gave me a quick, shaky kiss, then hit the floor where the rest of the hopefuls had gathered while I stayed by the wall with the squad. Joe casually pushed himself away and took a seat too. Chandra and I exchanged a hopeful glance, though what *she* was hoping for I had no idea. I just wanted Daniel to make it. I knew I probably should have cared that high-quality girls and guys would make the squad, but let's be honest. I wanted my man on the team. So sue me!

"Okay, everyone. The judges have made their decisions," Coach said, standing in front of the crowd with her clipboard raised. My heart beat an insane rhythm. Was Daniel's name somewhere on that clipboard? "It wasn't easy, but we've decided to take four guys this season."

Daniel and I looked at each other. Four out of eight. A fifty-fifty chance. I looked at each guy in the room, gauging who might have scored higher than Daniel. Charlie Novak? Not possible. He'd messed up the words and cursed in front of the judges. Jonah Trian? Not too sure. His arms had been kind of rubbery, but he was loud and had a lot of energy . . .

Oh, God. I just didn't know.

"But first," Coach said, "our new female members are . . . Shira Citron, Wendy Stewart and Ally Stevenson."

I smiled as the girls shouted and hugged happily. They were all juniors who had tried out with me and Mindy back in the fall. All of them were good then and all of them had improved this time around.

"Our two alternates are Veronica Hayes and Chastity Waldman."

"Yes," Sage said under her breath. Veronica and Chastity were two of her good friends. Two minions of the devil, in other words. They didn't even have the decency to look happy. I guess alternate wasn't good enough for them.

"Our four new male members are . . ."

I crossed my fingers behind my back. I tried to cross my toes, but they were too tightly bound into my sneakers. I would've crossed my eyes if part of me wasn't still afraid they would stay that way, as my mother had warned me two hundred thousand times that they would.

Daniel, Daniel, Daniel, I thought. *Daniel, Daniel, Daniel.*

"Joseph Trung, Steven Schwinn—"

"Yay!" Jaimee cried quietly. She and Steven had been friends since they were in Pampers. And I was happy for her and Steven. I was. But at the same time, my heart felt acidic. Only two spots left.

"Terrell Truluck—"

"Dammit," Tara said through her teeth.

I was actually surprised. Terrell had a great tryout, sure, but I had thought that Coach would keep him off the squad just because of the potential discipline problem. He was, at that very moment, doing a seated cabbage patch and making everyone around him either laugh or squirm.

"And finally," Coach said.

Come on! I thought. *Daniel, Daniel, Daniel. Daniel, Daniel, Daniel . . .*

"Daniel Healy."

"Yes!" I shouted at the top of my lungs. After a stunned silence, everyone laughed. Oops. Guess that was a little bit over-the-top. I turned fire-engine red, but couldn't stop smiling anyway. Who cared? Daniel had made the squad! He was a cheerleader. We were a cheer couple!

Okay. I had to stop now before I seriously started grossing myself out.

"The rest of you, thank you so much for your hard work," Coach Holmes said. "We hope to see you again next time. Will the new squad please stay for a brief meeting?"

Daniel slapped hands with Terrell as they stood, then turned around and allowed me to basically fling myself at him. I hugged him so hard, I knocked my own breath out of me.

"You did it!" I said. "You're a cheerleader!"

"Yeah I am!" Daniel shouted. He placed me on the floor and we grinned goofily at each other. "This is gonna be so cool."

"I know!" Already I was imagining long bus rides cuddled together in the backseat, paint fights during banner-making sessions, coming down from a basket toss and falling into Daniel's arms. Much more attractive than falling into Chandra's, I must say. I mean, I liked the girl, but come on. "So very, very cool."

• • •

"One plate of chili cheese fries for the bravest guys on the planet," I announced. The moment I dropped the heaping plateful of greasy food onto the table, Daniel and Steven dove right into the mound-o'-carbs as if it were their last meal. Jaimee leaned back into her vinyl seat like she was in mortal peril should she get any chili on her person.

39

"Take it easy," she said, scrunching her nose.

"Don't worry. Guys have stomachs of steel," Steven said, sucking on his Coke.

After our meeting with Coach Holmes, the entire squad had adjourned to Dolly's—a semi-outdoor beachfront diner that was SDH's primary hangout—and had basically taken over the place. Squad members lounged all over, taking up various booths and tables. In the corner Terrell and Joe shouted and laughed over the ancient pinball machine while Karianna, Lindsey and Sage and her minions, Veronica and Chastity, hovered nearby, cheering the boys on. Colorful Christmas lights were strung all around the place and a fiber-optic tree blinked red, then green, then red again above the cash register. Dolly herself stood behind the counter, Santa hat set at a jaunty angle on her head, watching one of the many Rudolph specials on her tiny TV.

Daniel slid over on the cracked plastic seat so that I could join them. A cool breeze blew through the open wall and I shivered, wrapping my arms around myself. Whenever the sun went down, it felt *slightly* more like Christmastime around here. Of course, the crashing surf in the background was a constant reminder that my imaginary Toto and I weren't in Jersey anymore.

"Hey, you cold?" Daniel asked, slipping out of his varsity jacket. I smiled gratefully as he draped it over my shoulders.

"Thanks," I said, beaming.

I loved wearing his jacket. Sometimes I was just *such* a girl.

As I pulled it closer to me, I noticed that while the little winged sneaker was still in place on the sleeve—representing Daniel's spot on the track team—he'd had the wrestling patch removed. Technically, this was Daniel's football jacket—it had a football and his number on the back—but multisports athletes usually had these patches representing their various talents added to the sleeves.

I, for example, was hoping that come spring, my cheerleading jacket would have a tennis racket sewn onto the sleeve. If I made the team.

"Hey. Maybe you should get a megaphone and put it here," I teased, touching the spot where the wrestler had been. There were still tiny holes in the leather from where the thread had been yanked out.

Daniel laughed. "Yeah. Maybe," he said sarcastically.

I blinked. Okay, maybe I had been semi-joking, but I felt a rush of hot irritation at his tone. Did he have to dismiss the idea so completely? And so snarkily?

"What?" I said. "You *are* a cheerleader."

Daniel reddened slightly and took a long sip from his straw. I glanced at Jaimee. Why did Daniel suddenly look ill?

"Yeah, but it might not be the wisest thing to, you know, *advertise* it," Steven put in.

"That's all I'm saying," Daniel added.

"Way to have squad pride," I said grumpily, grabbing a fry.

"No! It's not like that," Daniel said. "It's like if you . . . I don't know . . . what if you tried out for the wrestling team? Would you walk around advertising that you were a girl wrestler?"

"Yeah! I would!" Jaimee and I said in unison.

"I would be proud of myself for breaking down barriers," I said resolutely.

"Okay, well, I *am* proud of myself," Daniel said, munching on a fry. "I just . . . don't feel the need to shove my pride in everyone's faces."

My brow creased in consternation. I was definitely missing something here. I mean, I knew he was going to have a hard time with some of the guys thanks to his cheerleader status, but why participate in a sport if you were then going to try to hide the fact that you were on the team? I mean, he couldn't pretend that he *wasn't* a cheerleader any more than I could pretend I wasn't a brunette.

"I don't under—"

"Yo! Healy! Get your butt over here!" Terrell shouted from the corner. "I just beat your high score!"

"You did not, you loser!" Daniel shouted back. "Excuse me. I gotta go over there," he told us.

As I slid out of the booth to let him out, I could tell he was relieved to be out of the conversation. Personally, I would have rather gotten to the bottom of that one. But I supposed it could wait for another time.

"Sit down, Annisa. Relax," Steven said, draping both arms along the back of his seat. "It's supposed to be a party."

"Yeah. I know," I said. "So are you psyched for your first practice?" I asked with a mischievous smile.

"Beyond," Steven replied. "I can't wait to start throwing you ladies around."

"Me neither," I replied, sliding back into my seat. "It's gonna be so cool having that extra power on the team."

"You know it," Steven said, flexing his arms.

I laughed and was just about to snag another fry when Tara Timothy dropped down next to me.

"So. This sucks," she said.

So much for the relaxing thing.

"What?" Jaimee asked.

Tara glared at Steven, who was still flexing.

"And that's my cue," Steven said, dropping his arms and grabbing one last fry as he jumped up.

"What's the matter?" I asked Tara. "We have a great new squad, everyone's having fun. Get on board the happy train already."

"Yeah. You see a great new squad. I see disaster waiting to happen."

"You know, you are way too negative to be a cheer-leader," I said.

Phoebe slid into the seat across from Tara and blew out a sigh. "No, she's right," she said. "Check this out." She lifted her chin toward the corner and Tara and I turned around to look.

Joe and Lindsey were standing by the wall near the pin-ball machine and Lindsey was clearly flirting—touching Joe's arm, looking up at him with wide eyes, flipping her long blonde hair. His expression was, as usual, impassive, but she just kept right on working it, testing out her best material. Then Karianna came over, hips swaying, and handed Joe a strawberry shake. She slipped right in between him and Lindsey, totally commandeering his attention. And by that I mean he actually looked at her. Lindsey leaned back against the wall in a huff and shot a look of death at Karianna's back. Meanwhile, over by the pinball machine, Veronica and Kimberly were gazing at Terrell like he was the second coming of Taye Diggs.

"I think it's safe to say that cheerleading is not going to be anyone's top priority this season," Tara said, facing for-ward again.

"It'll be mine," Jaimee protested earnestly.

Just then, K. C. Lawrence and a couple of his friends from the wrestling team walked through the door, all slick and freshly showered after practice.

"Omigod! K. C. Lawrence," Jaimee said, reddening. "Let me out," she said to Phoebe.

Phoebe simply stared at her. "Hello, one-eighty."

"Come on! Come on! Let me out!" Jaimee pleaded.

Ever so slowly—and just to torture Jaimee—Phoebe pushed herself out of the booth and stepped aside so that Jaimee could scramble over to K.C.'s table. Two seconds after she arrived there, Sage, Lindsey and Chastity were there as well, crowding in with the guys, giggling at their jokes. Phoebe sat back down with a huff.

"Yeah. Her mind's on cheerleading," Tara said.

"It's like they're all groupies or something," I put in.

Over in the corner Terrell cheered some stupendous achievement of pinball primacy and a few of the girls squealed in delight. Somehow I had never before realized exactly how boy-crazy some of my squad mates were. And if the eighteen girls on the squad starting going after the four guys on the squad, things were not going to be pretty. And none of them better even *think* about going after *my* man, 'cause then I'd have to get medieval on these blondes.

Sorry. Jealousy-induced brain spasm.

Anyway, there could be a lot of rifts in the making around here. Maybe Tara was right. Maybe we had just welcomed the perfect poison onto the squad.

But then I heard Daniel laugh, and when I turned around and saw his heart-stopping smile, I knew everything was going to be fine. How could a person that perfect be poison? We would figure this thing out. It was just going to take some time, some adjustment.

This coed squad thing was going to be great.

• • •

"And now . . . coming to the center mat . . . wrestling at one hundred fifty pounds . . . give it up, Sand Dune fans, for your very own K! C! Lawrence!!!"

I jumped to my feet with the rest of the SDH crowd to shout for K.C., waving one of the blue-and-yellow mini-poms the spirit club had handed out before the meet. As K.C. made his way to the center mat to meet his opponent, he looked almost Cro-Magnon. The tightness of his blue jumpsuit made his arms look huge and his head and mouth guards distorted his features. At the other end of the bleachers the Clearwater High School fans booed his arrival. Then *we* booed *them*. Down below, K.C. didn't seem to notice any of it. He shook hands with the stout, crew-cut-sporting opponent and smiled through the plastic in his mouth.

"Do you miss it?" I asked Daniel as we sat.

He lifted his shoulders. "A little. But it was a lot of pressure, being out there one-on-one against someone else," he said. "I think I'm more of a team player."

"Me too," Mindy said. She scrunched the strands of her mini-pom between her palms to fluff it up. "That's why cheerleading tryouts always freaked me out. Being out there alone?" She gave a little shudder.

"Totally," Daniel agreed.

"Shh!" Bethany scolded from Mindy's far side. "I'm trying to concentrate!"

Behind us, Jaimee, Chandra and Autumn laughed, and as the ref blew the whistle to start the match, I could barely contain my glee. This was so great, being here with my friends and my boyfriend, sucking in all the kinetic, competitive energy in the air. Even if that air was a tad moist and sour with the stench of twenty years' worth of stale sweat. The Clearwater High gym could have used a little more ventilation, that's all I'm sayin'.

But no matter. It wasn't like it was keeping anyone away. The stands on our side were awash in light blue and yellow while the Clearwater stands were a sea of dark blue and white. Everyone on either side sat forward, eager to see K.C., the famous Junior Olympian, in action. It was one of those perfect movie moments. Those moments I resolved to take a mental snapshot of and remember forever.

Down below, K.C. and crew-cut boy crouched and faced each other, circling the center of the mat as they assessed the competition. They circled. And circled. And circled. But no one seemed eager to make the first move. I could feel the people around me growing more and more restless.

"Why doesn't K.C. do something?" I whispered to Daniel. Wrestling was not a sport I knew much about.

"He likes to let the other guy take the plunge," Daniel whispered back. "That's just his style. But it looks like this kid knows that."

"Come on! Grab him already!" Bethany shouted.

A bunch of people laughed and at that moment, K.C. lunged forward. A few people gasped as he upended crew-cut boy and sent him sprawling on the ground. I wasn't sure if Bethany's shout had momentarily distracted K.C.'s opponent, but whatever the case, K.C. *had* made the first move and had gotten the upper hand. Within two seconds he had crew-cut boy tangled into a pretzel.

There was an audible crack of joints and the crowd responded with a group wince.

"Yeah. That I don't miss," Daniel said, grinding his teeth.

"I don't think I could have handled watching you do this," I said.

Daniel nodded. "Cheerleading was definitely the better option."

I smiled. It was nice to hear him say that. Especially after that whole megaphone-on-the-jacket thing. I slipped my hand into Daniel's as, down below, the ref slammed the mat with his palm.

"Pin! Sand Dune! Win! Sand Dune!"

The crowd went nuts. All the Sand Dune High fans in attendance jumped to their feet. I was a little slower on the uptake. I grabbed Daniel's arm and hoisted myself up.

"What just happened?" I asked, trying to see over the heads of the people in front of me. A few fists were raised in the air, but I couldn't tell who they belonged to.

"K.C. just won," Daniel told me as he applauded.

My brow knit. "Just like that?"

"He's that good," Daniel responded.

"Oh."

Everyone sat down again and I felt a little deflated. That hadn't been all that exciting. Where was the drama? The struggle?

"They didn't even grunt once," Bethany said morosely, echoing my thoughts.

K.C. slapped hands with a few guys on the bench and suddenly I got an idea. An idea that perked me up considerably.

"Hey. You ready to put your money where your mouth is?" I asked Daniel, nudging his leg.

"What do you mean?" he said.

"I mean, you're a cheerleader now. It's time to start acting like one."

"But . . . the match is over," Daniel replied, gesturing at the empty mat. "They're on a break."

"Yeah, but K.C. deserves our appreciation, don't you think?" Mindy asked, getting the drift.

"Little K.C. chant?" I suggested, glancing at Autumn, Chandra and Jaimee behind us.

"Sounds like a plan."

"Aw, yeah," Chandra said.

"What're you doing?" Daniel asked, blanching.

"You're doing it too," I told him.

Together, Mindy, Chandra, Jaimee, Autumn and I started to chant, "K.C.!" Two claps. "K.C!" Two claps. "K.C.!" Two claps. "K.C.!" Two claps.

Chandra stood up and dragged me to my feet from behind. She turned around and gestured to the crowd as she chanted, urging them to their feet. I pulled on Daniel's jacket until he was forced to get up off his butt too. Bethany, of course, sank lower in her seat and hid her face with her hand.

"K.C.!"

Bam, bam.

"K.C.!"

Bam, bam.

Soon we had managed to bring most of the Sand Dune crowd into it. At first Daniel was a reluctant participant, but he started to grin when some other guys joined in and he gradually grew louder and louder.

"K.C.!" we shouted, laughing. "K.C.!"

Higher up in the stands, Tara, Phoebe, Whitney, Felice and Erin joined in. Then the other girls on the squad, peppered throughout the stands, got their neighbors into it as well.

As we chanted, K.C. turned bright red on the bench. He shook his head and grinned, trying to ignore us, but we made it completely impossible. The Clearwater guys looked up at us in irritated awe, but we just kept chanting and chanting and chanting. Finally, K.C. stood up and raised his arm to the crowd sheepishly. Everyone cheered and shouted and stomped.

"Thanks. Thank you," K.C. mouthed, waving.

Then, finally, he dropped back on the bench again and ducked his head. I would have felt bad for him if he wasn't grinning like a little kid on Christmas morning.

"Now, if I had ever gotten *that* kind of reaction, I would probably miss wrestling more," Daniel said as we sat down and the crowd finally quieted.

"See? It's fun, right?" I said. "Making people feel that good?"

Daniel grinned. "I could get used to it."

I smiled triumphantly at Mindy. We were going to turn this kid into a real cheerleader yet.

The basketball teams had Mondays off, so we had all gathered in the bleachers of the gym after classes for our first boy-girl practice. We had been sitting there for five minutes or so, gabbing away about our weekend activities, but we all fell silent at Coach's entrance. Basically because she had the most chiseled man ever to walk the face of the earth trailing behind her.

At least that was why the girls fell silent.

"Whoa. Who's the hottie?" Sage asked.

"Everyone, I'd like you to meet a friend of mine!" Coach Holmes announced as the pair stopped in front of us. "This is Coach Rincon."

"How is everyone today?" Rincon said, clasping his quite large hands together. Instantly his biceps bulged.

"Damn," Chandra muttered.

I might have echoed that sentiment if Daniel hadn't been sitting right behind me. Coach Rincon was Calvin Klein model gorgeous, with deeply tan skin, jade green eyes and dimples you could swim in. He had brown hair with golden highlights and long bangs that fell perfectly over his brows. A single diamond stud sparkled in one ear. And his arms? Don't even get me started. All I'll say is, that tight T-shirt should have been outlawed on an upper bod like that.

"Rincon was my stunting partner at Penn State," Coach said.

"Lucky girl," Lindsey whispered, earning a few giggles.

Rincon winked at her. I was impressed when she didn't have a heart attack—both from being caught and from being winked at.

"He has graciously offered to spend the next couple of weeks helping me teach you guys some stunting skills," Coach continued. "So let's give him a big Sand Dune welcome."

We all applauded and a couple of the girls threw in some hoots and hollers. Rincon placed his hand to his chest and gave an honored little bow.

"That guy could throw me to France if he wanted to," Sage said.

"Why don't you take a second and let them get to know you?" Coach suggested to her new partner in crime. "I've gotta get something from my office."

"Sure," Rincon said with a nod. His nod was even hot. How that's possible, I have no idea, but I saw it with my own eyes.

Coach walked out and Rincon smiled slowly at us. Hearts broke all over the bleachers. Daniel shifted uncomfortably and I wondered if the rise in my body heat was palpable. Had to get control of that.

"Well, as your coach mentioned, my name is Leo Rincon—"

"Oooh . . . *Leo*," Lindsey whispered all huskily.

"I grew up in Miami and I cheered at Penn State," he said. "After graduation I worked in the corporate world for a while, but that turned out to be boring as sin," he said with a mischievous glint in his eye that made Lindsey sigh audibly. "So now I am the head cheerleading coach at Florida State. I love my job, but when Deirdre called me, I had to come up right away to help. You never turn down a request from Deirdre."

"Deirdre?" Sage said. "What kind of parents saddle a girl with a name like Deirdre?"

Yeah. Like *Sage* was such a winner.

"Oops. Were you not supposed to know that?" Rincon said. "That'll have to be our little secret."

The girls all giggled at that, and Terrell scoffed. I had a feeling the guys were kind of threatened by Rincon.

Coach returned then, kicking the door open because her arms were wrapped around the props box—a cardboard box that was covered with blue and yellow paper megaphones. All the veterans perked up slightly and there was an excited murmur that made me cringe. I had no love for the props box myself, being that the last time I saw it, the thing had spurred a good couple weeks of personal misery. It had contained several suggestions from persons unknown (most likely Tara and Sage) that I dye my hair blonde for uniformity before nationals. Suggestions that had made me paranoid and irritable, which then made everyone around me annoyed. Good times.

Yeah, I hated the props box. Everyone else, however, worshipped the darn thing.

"Everything going okay?" she asked Rincon.

"We like each other already," our new coach replied.

"Aw, Coach. Did you bring us a present?" Terrell asked, eyeing the box.

The boys all snickered. Everyone except for Steven, who had witnessed the last reading of the props box and seen me freak out. I squirmed. Sarcastic jokes were not the way to get on Coach Holmes' good side. But she smiled at him, clearly deciding to let it slide.

"This, for those of you who don't already know, is a props box," Coach said, thrusting both hands at the box like she was a model at a car show, displaying the latest Fast-and-Furious-mobile. "Whenever you have a compliment for another member of the team, or a suggestion on how to make our squad even better, you write it down and put it in the box. Anonymously, of course. Halfway through the season we'll open it up and see what everyone has to say."

Terrell snorted a laugh. Every girl on the squad turned around to glare at him. Even the ones who had spent all of Friday night flirting with him. You did not mock the props box.

"What? It's a joke, right?" he said, spreading his hands wide. Met with silence, he raised his eyebrows. "It's *not* a joke?"

"No, Mr. Truluck. I'm afraid it's not," Coach said impatiently.

Terrell scoffed again. "What is this, a team or a Brownie troop?"

"I don't do Brownie troops," Joe said.

Oh, they were so very dead. Suddenly I saw antlers sprout out of Terrell's and Joe's heads as Coach chased after them sporting an orange hunter's jacket and wielding a shotgun.

"Listen up, people. We take the props box seriously," Coach said, hands on hips. "Basketball season is a long season with a lot of games and a lot of practices. Eventually the squad tends to get unmotivated and certain people slack off, leaving others to pick up the pieces. For the past few years, that has resulted in blowups and fights between squad mates. Well, this year, I'm hoping to nip that in the bud. Once we start to feel a little tension, we'll open up the props box, read the contents and get psyched up again."

"It's very therapeutic," Autumn said.

"I don't know about you guys, but I'm *always* psyched," Terrell said casually, leaning back on his elbows.

Daniel laughed and Steven and Joe hid their smiles behind their hands. Tara had a serious "I told you so" face on, but she had enough of a self-preservation instinct to direct it at the gym floor rather than at Coach.

"Are you?" Coach said, crossing her arms over her chest. "Good. Then maybe you and your friends back there wouldn't mind going into the wrestling gym and bringing back their extra mats so we can get to work in here. And while you're doing that, you'll be missing our warm-up, so when you get back, I'm thinking you should do double push-ups, triple crunches and ten extra laps around the gym."

Now it was the girls' turn to snicker.

"Crunches?" Daniel said.

"I don't do crunches," Joe said.

"You do now," Rincon said. "Crunches are key. We have to build up your core strength for stunting. I think the guys will be doing at least a couple hundred today, am I right?" he asked, looking to Coach Holmes for confirmation.

A couple hundred? This guy meant business.

"Sounds good." Coach Holmes smirked. "You didn't think you were joining a Brownie troop, did you, Healy?"

Silence. My neck prickled with heat on Daniel's behalf.

"Did you?" Coach repeated.

"No, Coach," Daniel said loudly.

"Good. Now, the four of you. Go," she said.

The guys scrambled up and loped down the bleachers past us. From the uniform slump of their shoulders you might have thought they were surprised and disappointed to learn they were actually going to have to work out. *Had* they thought they were joining a Brownie troop? What did they think we did all afternoon? Trade beauty secrets? Wait until our first trip to the weight room. These guys were in for a serious wake-up call.

"Told you she'd whip them into shape," Chandra said under her breath as the other girls whispered and giggled. Coach slid a no-nonsense stare our way and everyone instantly clammed up.

"The rest of you, push-ups," Coach said firmly, narrowing her eyes. *"Now."*

• • •

"How much longer are we going to do this?" Terrell said softly.

"I think it's kind of fun," Sage replied flirtatiously.

She kicked up her feet and jumped off the third bleacher into Terrell's arms. He caught her effortlessly, with his arms and hands in perfect position, which wasn't all that shocking, considering we had each practiced it at least fifty times under Coach Rincon's watchful eyes. Phoebe went next, jumping into Joe's outstretched arms. On the other side of the gym, Tara and Coach Holmes worked on teaching some of the new girls a few of the more popular cheers while Chandra and the others went over basic all-girl stunts. Of course I, like Sage, enjoyed being right where I was, no matter how repetitive the activity. Because when I stepped to the end of the bleacher, Daniel was waiting for me.

"Ready?" I asked.

"Ready," he replied with a smile.

I jumped up, locked my legs and came down right in his arms.

"Perfect!" Rincon said.

Couldn't have agreed more.

Daniel smiled and placed me down on my feet. Jaimee was just about to do her jump with Steven when Rincon clapped his hands.

"I think we all have the cradling position down," he said. "Let's—"

"I could do it in my sleep," Terrell said, not so quietly. Sage giggled and touched his arm. Unbelievable. She was flirting with Terrell. Right in front of her ex-boyfriend, who also happened to be her *current* boyfriend's brother. What was it with this girl? It was like whenever she was around guys, she developed boyfriend-related amnesia.

"Terrell, is it?" Rincon said.

In the background the rest of the girls started up the hello cheer, their voices and claps echoing through the gym.

"Yeah," Terrell said.

"Good. Terrell, you and your partner will be first," Rincon said, stepping over to the blue-and-gold mat behind him. "To the mat, please."

"Now you're talking," Terrell said, rubbing his hands together.

"The name's Sage," Sage told Rincon as she sauntered past him. "In case you were wondering."

Classy. She was flirting with him too. Thankfully, Rincon didn't flirt back. That would have been too gross to handle.

"Thank you, Sage," he said flatly. Then he turned and shouted across the room. "Coach Holmes! Can I see you over here for a moment?"

Coach said a few words to Tara, then jogged over. "What's up?"

"I'd like to demonstrate a chair sit, if you don't mind," Rincon said.

"Great. Let's do it," Coach replied.

"Everyone watch how this works," Rincon said. "Guys, pay attention to my hands, my stance, my eyes. When stunting, we keep our eyes on our partners at all times. No exceptions."

Coach Holmes stepped in front of him and he placed his hands on her small waist. She reached back and braced her hands on his wrists, which were already taped up with what looked like gauze and first aid tape.

"One, two," Rincon said.

Coach bent her knees and popped up, as if weightless, into the air. She landed perfectly with her butt on Rincon's palm, one knee raised, her arms in a high V. Across the room, Chandra whistled and everyone cheered. Coach Holmes was the goods.

"Nice," Daniel said.

"This is gonna be so cool," I agreed, the butterflies in my stomach fluttering with excitement.

I glanced over at Terrell and Sage, who were supposedly *so psyched* about stunting. He, for some reason, was inspecting her palm and she was giggling and blinking up at him.

As Coach cradled out into the position we'd all been practicing, Terrell whispered something to Sage and Sage doubled over laughing. Terrell grabbed for her waist and Sage squealed and whirled away, batting at his hand. I exchanged a look of doom with Phoebe. These two were both so wrapped up in their flirt fest that they were entirely oblivious to the fact that the whole gym was silent and we were all staring at them.

So very uncool.

"Barnard! Truluck!" Coach Holmes barked, her nostrils flaring.

They both stopped and looked up. Sage had the intelligence, at least, to go ashen.

"I think Coach Rincon's instructions were pretty clear," Holmes said. "You were supposed to be watching the stunt."

"Sorry, Coach," Sage said, snapping her feet together and placing her hands behind her back.

"I hope so, Barnard, because you and your partner there will be sitting out the rest of the stunting practice," Coach Holmes said.

"What? Why?" Terrell protested.

"Terrell, what did I tell you at the beginning of practice?" Coach Rincon said, his jaw clenched. Man took his stunting seriously. "Safety, attentiveness, awareness at all times. You just completely missed the demonstration of the stunt I was about to teach you because you were too busy tickling your partner."

Phoebe hid a laugh behind her hand and I bit my lip.

"I saw it," Terrell said, lifting his chin. Even though his cluelessness was evident in his eyes.

"No, you didn't," Rincon said.

"Sit down, please, you two," Coach Holmes said calmly.

"But I—"

"Sit. *Down.*"

I think every dog and young child in the state of Florida responded to the no-nonsense strength of that order. Sage sighed, but did as she was told. Terrell looked for a moment like he was going to argue further, but Daniel caught his eye and surreptitiously shook his head. Finally Terrell huffed by us and dropped onto the bottom bleacher, shoving his legs out and crossing his arms over his chest like a petulant five-year-old who'd just been put in time-out.

Honestly, I was starting to wonder why Daniel hung out with this guy. But then, I usually enjoyed hanging out with Terrell too. Back when he was just funny cutup Terrell who wasn't constantly wasting everyone's time and irritating my coach to no end.

"Daniel, Annisa, on the mat, please," Coach said.

We exchanged a determined look and I knew that Daniel, at least, was ready to work. Good. Because I was more than eager to start learning these stunts. They were definitely going to bring a whole new dimension to the team.

That was if we could all manage to concentrate long enough to get it together.

• • •

"We're going to do it this time. We are," I said firmly.

"I've got it this time. I swear," Daniel said through his teeth. "I am going to catch you."

Right. Where had I heard that one before? Oh, yeah. The last twenty times we'd tried the chair sit. Unsuccessfully. I nodded, but inside I was all out of resolution. Daniel may have been nervous, but he had no idea what it was like to keep seeing the ground rushing up at me over and over and over again. To watch Sage laughing at me openly. To have my stomach swoop up above my heart so many times, I was pretty sure I'd never be able to process solid food again.

Plus, Joe, who was supposed to be our extra spotter, had zoned out about ten minutes ago. Every once in a while he'd mutter something under his breath and I could have sworn I heard numbers in there. Was he doing math problems in his head to keep from falling asleep from boredom?

"It's okay. The first time is never easy," Rincon said. "But I promise you, once you break this barrier, everything else is going to come much quicker. All you need is one successful stunt to get your confidence back."

"That sounds good," I said. I glanced over my shoulder at Daniel. "Doesn't that sound good?"

"Definitely," he replied with a hopeful smile and a determined nod.

"Okay, get set," Rincon said, stepping back and crossing his arms over his chest. He placed his hands under his biceps, which just made them bulge even bigger. "Whenever you're ready."

I gripped Daniel's wrists. He set his stance behind me. "Okay," he said. "One, two!"

I flew straight up into the air.

Knee up, lock your arms. Concentrate . . . concentrate . . .

I felt Daniel's palm under my seat. All the blood in my body rushed to my face. I was up!

And then I came sliding right back down. And my butt? Well, that hit Daniel's face. My *butt* slid right over Daniel's *face!* We're talking nose to posterior here, people. Why, oh, why had I ever thought that this was going to be romantic?

I mean, why not just strip me naked and throw me into center court in the middle of a pep rally?

Joe put his hands out halfheartedly to catch me, but this had already happened ten million times and we all knew I didn't need his help. I just landed right back down on my sore feet. My face had long since taken on a permanent red hue, so I couldn't even blush in my embarrassment. I felt more like crying.

Terrell and Sage groaned audibly. Like they were so totally bored. My scowl could have leveled cities. I'd like to see them get up here and try this.

On second thought, maybe not. Because if they did it on the first try or something, that would be a humiliation from which I might never recover.

"Sorry. Sorry," Daniel said. I could hear the intense frustration in his voice. "I just . . . I'm afraid of hurting you."

"You're not gonna hurt me," I told him.

Hello? My butt making contact with your nose is a lot more painful than any injury could ever be. So try catching me!

"And besides, this is a sport. If I do get a little bruised, it comes with the territory."

"Yeah, dude. Ever worried if one of the linebackers you smacked into was gonna get black and blue?" Terrell asked from the cheap seats.

"It's a good point," Rincon said. "It doesn't totally apply, since Annisa *is* on your team and safety comes first. But if you're worried about hurting her when you catch her, don't. You *are* catching her on the most padded part of the body."

"Especially on her," Sage said.

Phoebe whacked her leg as I turned a nice shade of royal purple. Okay, so maybe I *could* still blush in embarrassment.

61

"You two just need to lose the fear," Rincon said, determined. "Daniel, you're not going to hurt her. Annisa, you are not going to fall. Just visualize yourself doing it, and you'll do it."

Yeah. Because I had magical powers. Just like the chicks on *Charmed*. In my spare time I also enjoyed morphing into other people, orbing to foreign lands and blowing things up with my hands.

Visualize, I thought. *Visualize . . .*

"We can do this, Daniel," I said, looking him dead in the eye. "Pretend it's not me. Pretend this is just a football drill or something. Coach won't let you play this weekend unless you catch the girl."

Daniel smirked. "Got it."

"Okay, get set," Rincon said.

I turned around. I placed my hands on Daniel's wrists. *We can do it. We can do it. We can do it.*

I stared straight ahead. I was not coming down this time. I was not.

"Okay." Daniel's voice had taken on a new, fearless tone. "One, two!"

I flew up into the air. I felt Daniel's hand under my bottom, but this time, he held on. Holy acrobatics, he held on! I threw my arms into the high V. Daniel's other hand suddenly found my lower ankle and steadied me.

"Yes!" I shouted.

Phoebe, Jaimee, Steven, Sage, Terrell and Joe all whooped and hollered. The rest of the squad stopped what they were doing and I heard a couple of gasps of surprise when they saw me up there. Below me, Daniel was solid as a rock, and

I was so high in the air, I was eye level with the upper bleachers.

"Nice work!" Rincon said, clapping his hands. Coach Holmes jogged over and looked up at me, beaming with pride.

"Nice work, you two!" she said.

"Thanks," I replied giddily.

We had done it. We were on our way. Partner-stunting championships, here we come!

"Okay, time to cradle out," Rincon said.

My heart slammed into my ribs. Oh, crap. Cradle out? From *here*? How? How the heck were we supposed to do that?

I looked down uncertainly and felt Daniel's arm waver. My butt tilted. I started to slide. Then everything happened in fast forward. I shouted in surprise, Daniel's arm collapsed, I slid down his front, he caught my waist, I stepped on his foot, he doubled over, and we both went down in a tangle of limbs, taking Joe with us.

Ow. That kind of hurt.

Slowly, I rolled over, removing Daniel's hand from my face. Wincing, I looked up at my coaches. They both had semi-blank expressions on as they stared down at the human pretzel.

"Yeah. We're gonna need a little more work then," Coach Holmes said.

Rincon nodded. "Yeah. Looks like."

Oops.

Okay, what do I need? What do I need . . . ?

I stood at my locker before first period, staring into its light blue depths at the stack of books in the top portion, completely blanking on my morning classes. I had woken up in a fog that morning. After a late night standing in front of my full-length mirror practicing cheers and *visualizing* stunts, my sleep had been peppered with freaky nightmares with absolutely no foundation in anything (something to do with a duck-headed dog chasing me through a swamp into my grandmother's house, where all my teachers from every school I'd ever been to were waiting to give me tests), and even after a bowl of Cap'n Crunch and a brisk walk to school (since I was late), I still could barely keep my eyes open. What did I have second period? What was I supposed to have done for it? Where on earth was my brain?

To add injury to insult, my butt hurt. A lot. My tailbone throbbed so hard, it could have been a beacon trying to summon E.T. back to the home planet. But the good news was, Daniel and I had successfully mastered the chair sit and the cradle out. We'd done it perfectly at least a dozen times.

At least I think we had. Was it possible I had dreamt all that too?

"Okay, snap out of it, Annisa. You have the whole day ahead of you," I said to myself.

I knew people were staring at me in slightly disturbed confusion as they made their way to their classes, but I couldn't seem to wake myself up without talking to myself. I was already known all over school as a klutzy freak. Maybe now I would add space-case to my resume. Klutzy space-case freak. Had a certain ring to it.

Mornings suck, I thought. *Mornings totally suck.*

It was about the only coherent thought I could form.

Suddenly my locker slammed closed before my eyes. I was startled, but I didn't have the energy to flinch.

"You are so gonna love me!" Daniel announced, planting a kiss on my lips.

Well. That'll wake you up.

"Hey! Where were you this morning? I waited for like ten minutes," he said. He was wearing this aqua blue T-shirt that totally brought out his eyes. I could get lost in those eyes. Especially on a morning like this. I just wanted to cuddle up against him and take a nap.

Exciting, no?

"Brain fog," I told him flatly. "Do you know what I have second period?"

Daniel's adorable eyebrows came together. Yes, even his eyebrows are adorable. "Chemistry," he said. "Are you okay?"

"Chemistry! Yes!" I said, working my lock again. "And after that it's Spanish. Ah. It's all coming back to me now."

"You're a psycho, you know that?" Daniel said playfully, reaching out to tuck a wayward hair behind my ear.

"I'm aware," I replied. I popped open my locker and

started rooting around for my chemistry book. "So why, exactly, am I going to love you?"

Not that I don't already, I added silently.

His smile widened, sending my heart into a series of impressive flips. "I got your Christmas present," he said. "And it is perfect."

"Oooh! What is it?" I asked, waking up even more now. Nothing like the promise of a boyfriendly gift to get the blood pumping. It was better than a direct shot of Red Bull. Of course I had already bought Daniel's present a few weeks earlier. He was a huge classic rock fan and had recently gotten into the Rolling Stones, so I'd picked him up a Rolling Stones CD box set that I had raided half of my allowance savings to afford. But I hadn't teased him once about it. Mostly because I knew if I started and he wheedled, I would probably blurt it out and ruin the surprise.

"Can't tell you!" he said, loving the torture a little too much.

"Daniel!"

"I'd tell you, but then I'd have to kill you," he said with a shrug, walking away.

I slammed my locker and chased after him. "Come on! No fair!" I whined. "Give me a hint!"

At that moment, Christopher Healy, Bobby Goow and a couple of other guys from the football team came around the corner and nearly walked right into us. Christopher threw his hands up and backed away a few steps.

"Pardon me, *ladies*," he said pointedly, looking at Daniel. The other guys laughed and Daniel's face fell.

"Hey! It's Mini-Chris!" one of the guys from the wrestling team said. "Or should I call you Mini-Chris*tine*?"

"Shut up, loser," Daniel said.

"Oooooh. Don't get your panties all in a twist now, li'l sis," Christopher mocked, much to his friends' glee. "Wouldn't want you to throw a hissy fit right here in the hall-way."

Ugh! What a Neanderthal jerk. What year was he born, anyway? 1945? Not that everyone was a sexist in 1945, but, you know, I'm guessing there were a few more then than there are today.

I glanced at Daniel, willing him to formulate the perfect comeback, but he simply stood there, stock-still, his face growing blotchy and hot. No fair. One second he was hap-pily teasing me and the next he was miserable. All thanks to his own brother. I would never understand boys. Why did they enjoy making each other unhappy?

Oh, but wait. Girls did that too sometimes. Witness my first few weeks at school, being tortured by Tara Timothy.

"So, what're you two talking about? What to bring to the slumber party this weekend?" Lumberjack Bob asked, clasp-ing his hands under his chin, all wide-eyed and breathless.

"Bite me, Bobby," Daniel replied.

Okay, that was something. Maybe not the most inspired argument, but something.

"Tough words coming from a cheerleader," Bobby said, pitching his voice up an octave on the final word. "What're you gonna do next, high-kick me to death?"

Daniel looked mortified and miserable. I wondered why he stood there and took it. Why he didn't just walk away.

"Hey, bro, when do you get fitted for your miniskirt?" Christopher asked, smirking. "That's gonna be a proud moment for the family. I'm thinking I'll take some pictures to bring home to Dad."

All right. That was it.

"Leave him alone," I said.

Instantly all the guys looked at me. It was as if they had forgotten I was even there, but now that they remembered, the mirth was universal. "Oooh! The little girl's defending the little girl!"

"Little girl? Do you know how much guts it took for him to go in there and try out for the squad? Only a real man could do something like that," I said. "I know you couldn't," I added, looking Christopher up and down.

His eyes darkened and he stepped toward me. "Yeah, Annisa. He's a real man," he said, patting me on the shoulder. "You just keep telling yourself that when you guys are baking cookies together on your next date."

With that, the guys all cracked up and moved off, trailing one after the other past me so they could each have a chance to sneer in my face. I couldn't believe it. How could people be so immature and closed-minded? Was this not the twenty-first century we were living in?

"I don't know how you live with that guy," I said, turning to Daniel.

Instantly, the earth dropped out from underneath my feet. Daniel's eyes were full of humiliated anger and they were focused on me. Not his brother and his band of witless wonders, but me.

"Daniel?"

"What the hell was that?" he blurted. "Do you have any idea how much crap I'm gonna take for that?"

My mouth opened, but nothing came out other than a strained "I . . ."

"I can't have a girl defending my honor, Annisa! Especially not now!"

Oh, God. Oops. I'd broken the guy code. See? This was what happened when I was around. Stupid mouth. Had a mind of its own.

"I . . . I'm sorry," I said.

"Dammit," Daniel said under his breath.

I didn't know what to say. I hated that I had put that expression on his face. Well, *helped* put it there.

"Daniel, I'm really sorry," I said. "I told you . . . brain fog. I'm not thinking straight this morning."

Daniel sighed and looked at his feet. I was feeling kind of wistful for the playful banter of five minutes ago.

"It's all right. Just . . . don't do it again," Daniel said finally.

"I won't," I said. "I promise."

The warning bell rang and we both had to get to classes at opposite ends of the school.

"See you later?" I said, biting my bottom lip and raising my eyebrows. I was going for irresistibly cute. I'll admit it. I'm not above flirting for forgiveness.

But it didn't work.

"Yeah. See ya," Daniel said. Then he turned around and walked away without so much as a kiss on the forehead.

I could kill Christopher. Seriously. This was a great morning until he and his closed mind entered my world.

When my brain finally registered the fact that Daniel was not, in fact, coming back for a kiss, I turned and trudged off to class. The fog returned, but this time it took over my entire body. I had no idea how I was going to make it through an entire day of school *and* practice feeling like this.

It wasn't that I didn't understand how it worked. I did. Boys picked on other boys for being less than men. Happened all the time. Not that it was right, but it happened all the time. What I didn't understand was why I was expected to just go along with it. Why was Daniel allowed to stick up for me, but I wasn't allowed to stick up for him? Especially when he needed sticking up for?

Deep question. Definitely too deep for a girl in a morning fog.

• • •

I reached up to hang my favorite Hallmark Christmas ornament on our brand-new Christmas tree and a light, warm breeze wafted through the window, bringing with it the scent of tropical flowers. One of the little brass bells on the upper branches danced and tinkled. With a sigh, I dropped back onto the couch.

"This is just wrong," I said.

My father finally pulled his head out of one of our many huge boxes of ornaments. His graying hair stuck out straight over his ears and his glasses fell down from atop his head, coming to rest on the tip of his nose.

"What's just wrong?" he asked, pushing the glasses up toward his eyes and glancing into the box again. "Aha! Found another one! She can't fool me!" he cried, ripping the tissue paper off a decrepit old nutcracker ornament. It had one leg, half an arm and what appeared to be bite marks on its face.

We've never had a dog or a cat or anything, so where those marks came from, I had no idea.

"This!" I said, throwing my hands up toward the window. "How can I be expected to fully immerse myself in the Christmas spirit when I have warm breezes coming in through my living room windows? I mean, you put lights on a palm tree, Dad. That's just wrong."

"No. What's wrong is that your mother took them down," my dad said, lovingly hanging the battered nutcracker on a prominent branch.

"Right. That was very wrong of her," I agreed. "But Dad, look at you. You're wearing a Hawaiian shirt! Does that not strike you as odd? It's December and you're wearing a Hawaiian shirt!" My brow knit. "And a mightily unattractive one, I might add."

My dad was not known for Golden Hanger–worthy fashion sense, but this shirt brought him to new lows. It was covered with red and green flowers and had topless Santas hula dancing here and there all over it. They wore sunglasses and leis and grass skirts and the only Santa-esque details about them were their little Santa hats. I missed the days when my father had kept the AC cranked up to arctic levels so that we'd all feel more at home. My parents and I had spent our first two months as Florida residents sporting wool sweaters while people cruised by outside in top-down convertibles, half dressed, with zinc on their noses. At first I had hated it, but now it was Christmas and I wanted to be cold. Dad had sure picked the wrong time of year to give up *that* habit.

"Come on, kiddo. Don't let it get to you," my father said,

fishing out another ancient ornament. "The weather isn't important. The important thing is that we're all going to be together and that all of our other traditions are going to be unchanged."

"Right. Like our Christmas Eve snowball fight," I said grumpily.

"So instead we'll have a Christmas Eve dip in the pool," my father said. "A splash war."

Yeah. That's festive.

"Aha! Here's another!" my father cried, yanking out a plastic Santa with half a spotty beard.

"I don't know why you bother putting all this stuff up," I said, hoisting myself up off the couch. "You know Mom's just going to get up in the middle of the night and replace it all with new balls and things."

"Yes, your mother and I have different decorating styles when it comes to the holidays," my father said, lovingly hanging the ornament. "But it just goes to show that opposites attract. Besides, I think it's kind of fun, trying to sneak a few of these things by her."

Different decorating styles? More like polar opposite. His was tacky-traditional and colorful, with a huge emphasis on never throwing anything away—even the plastic lawn nativity set that had seen better days in, I don't know, the 1970s? Hers was upscale, classic, white lights, fir garland and red bows only, please. We all knew what their styles were, but neither of them would ever blast the other's tastes to his or her face, so instead they went all Navy SEAL on each other, switching up ornaments, wreaths and lighting schemes in the middle of the night or while the other was at work. I never knew which house I was coming home to at the end

of the day. Barnum and Bailey's Christmas at the Gob-
rowskis' or a Martha Stewart Holiday.

But my dad was right. It did make it kind of fun.

"All right. Hand me one of those butt-ugly elves," I said,
holding out a hand.

"That's my girl," my dad replied with a grin.

Suddenly I heard a rumble in the distance and for a
moment I thought it might be thunder. But it was too con-
sistent and there was no lightning. And then it got louder,
and closer, and closer, and louder, until it was clear it was
one loud-as-Armageddon motorcycle and it was . . . stopping
in front of our house.

My father and I exchanged a confused look and raced to
the window. Our jaws hit the windowsill in unison. Parking
a gleaming Harley in the driveway was none other than my
older brother, Gabe Gobrowski. He wore a silver-studded
leather jacket and torn jeans, and when he lifted off his helmet, his formerly well-coiffed red hair was shaggy and
gelled on top. But insane-o fashion choice of all? He was
sporting a mustache. An actual thick red mustache.

"Oh, I don't think so!" my father said. "Michella!"

"I see him!" my mother shouted, already racing down the
stairs. Her long red hair was down around her shoulders,
having just been brushed out after being pinned up all day
at work. She wore a pair of slim jeans, but her silk work shirt
was still on and it was all untucked and wrinkled, hanging
out sloppily—very un-Mom. She stuffed her feet into my
father's slippers as we all ran out the front door.

My heart flipped in glee. This was going to be good.
Every so often my brother liked to completely change his
style, keep people guessing, try on new personas. It used to

be he'd test something out for a few months before chang-ing it up again, but this year he was like a chameleon on speed. Every time I saw him, he was a whole new Gabe. Sometimes the parentals were down with his new style, some-times not. Now he looked like he'd just rolled off the set of *Orange County Choppers*. Apparently that was a "not."

"Gabriel Gobrowski!" my mother shouted.

"Mama!" Gabe cried, throwing his arms wide, still strad-dling the bike.

She stopped at the edge of the front walk. "*What* is *that?*" she shouted.

"It's my new ride," Gabe said, lovingly stroking the han-dlebars. "Sweet, isn't she?"

"Not that!" my mother shouted, taking a few steps for-ward. "That!"

She pointed at his mustache. I snorted a laugh.

"Just a little facial accessory," Gabe said with a shrug. "Makes me look tougher, don't you think?"

Actually, it kind of made him look like a disco star.

"Oh, honey!" my mother lamented, placing her hands on either side of his face. "What happened to your hair? And your tan? And that nice suede jacket you had the last time we saw you?"

Poor Mom. Apparently she had really hoped Gabe was going to stick with the metrosexual thing he'd been rocking at Thanksgiving. Not that I could blame her. She was a fash-ion plate herself, so Gabe dressing like he'd stepped right out of a *Queer Eye* episode must have made her very happy.

"Sorry, Ma," Gabe said. "That wasn't really me."

"And this is?" my mother said, shaking her head.

"For now," Gabe said.

"Gabriel, where's your car?" my father asked.

"Sold it," Gabe said nonchalantly, swinging his leg over the motorcycle. He had on some thick black boots with a serious tread. Mental note: keep bare toes out of Gabe's way. "Traded it in for this bad boy, actually. Anybody wanna go for a spin?"

"On that death trap? I don't think so," my mother said. "Gabe, one of these days you're really going to give me a heart attack, you know that, right?"

"Come on, Mama," Gabe cajoled. "I'm totally responsible with it."

"It's not you I'm worried about," my mom said. "It's every other psychotic, drunken, doing-their-makeup-in-the-rearview-mirror driver on the road."

"It's fine, really," Gabe said, clucking his tongue. "Why don't you let me take you out for a ride and I'll show you?"

"I'll go!" I said, raising a hand.

"No, you will not," my father said, jumping in. "*You* are over eighteen and we can't tell you what to do with your own life, but you are under no circumstances to take your sister out on that thing, do you understand me?" he asked Gabe.

"Uh . . . sure," Gabe said.

"Do *you* understand me?" my father asked me.

I nodded mutely. Even though it felt like just another one of the world's double standards to me. It was okay for the boy child to ride the hog, but heaven forbid the girl child goes out on the thing.

"All right, well, I'm going back inside to change," my

mother said, turning around. "A mustache," she muttered under her breath as she walked back to the house. "My baby grew a mustache."

At the door she paused, quickly snatched my father's cheesy Rudolph off the door and went inside.

"Dad, don't be mad," Gabe said. "I mean, look! It's a Harley."

"Contrary to popular belief, Gabriel, it is not every male's fantasy to own one of these things," my father said sternly. "And it's especially not *my* fantasy to have my kids driving around on them. Now if you say you're responsible with it, I'm sure you are, but that doesn't mean that your mother and I aren't going to worry every second you're on it."

Wow. Dad was really serious about this. Gabe and I looked at each other grimly.

"Okay, Dad," Gabe said finally. "But I swear I'll be careful."

"Okay," my father replied. "Annisa, why don't you help your brother with his things? Then you can both come inside and help me finish the tree."

With that my father turned and walked into the house. He never even hugged my brother hello or anything.

"Well. Merry freakin' Christmas," Gabe said.

"You know, you become a little bit more of a moron with every new personality you adopt," I told him. "You're going to need to quit soon or we're going to have a *Flowers for Algernon* situation on our hands."

Gabe narrowed his eyes. "Huh?"

I laughed. "You had to know Dad was going to hate this. He's Mr. Training Wheels. Mr. Safety Goggles. Mr. What's the Point of Roller Coasters. And you traded in the car he picked out for you without telling him? What were you thinking?"

"I got it. I got it," Gabe said moodily.

"Well, at least *I'm* glad to see you," I said, following him over to the bike.

The Harley *was* pretty sweet. Black and red and shiny all over. Too bad it was loud enough to spur disturbing-the-peace violations. Gabe opened up one of the side storage compartments and lifted out a black backpack. There was a Harley-Davidson patch sewn onto the back. Last time I saw him he'd been toting a silver-and-gray messenger bag. The time before that it was a yellow Billabong bag. Where he got the money for all this stuff, I had no idea. Maybe every time he adopted a new persona he sold all his old crap on eBay to finance all his new crap.

"You are?" he asked.

"Yeah. I need a guy's opinion on something," I said. "See, I was in the hallway with Daniel this morning and—"

"Ooh. Have a tiff with cheer boy?" he asked, walking around to the other compartment. Already I didn't like Biker Gabe. He was a little too sarcastically belligerent for my tastes.

"Ha-ha," I said. "But listen. His brother and these other guys were picking on him and he wouldn't say anything, so I jumped in and—"

"No," my brother said, slamming the compartment lid down. "No, you didn't."

"What?" I asked as my heart turned.

"Did you defend him? For being a cheerleader? To other guys?" he demanded. I had filled my brother in on the new squad last week on the phone. My face must have told all because Gabe dropped his head back. "Have I taught you nothing?"

I felt like my life was flashing before my eyes. Every older brother–younger sister chat we'd ever had—every piece of abstract advice he'd ever given me—played itself out in my head. I was pretty sure "defending cheerleader boyfriend's honor" had never come up.

Gabe walked around his bike, backpack in one hand, laundry bag in the other. Oh, to be a guy and only have to carry two bags home for an entire month.

"Listen, *A*," he said, loading a Tara Timothy's worth of disdain into that one vowel. "The guy has already emasculated himself enough. He doesn't need you making it worse."

Then he shook his head, as if he was just *so* at a loss, and trudged by me up the walk. So there it was. All guys *were* the same. Even the ones who changed their entire personalities once a month.

One second after Gabe made it through the door, my mother yanked it open again, hung a beautiful fir wreath with a red bow on a silver door hook, then slammed it.

Let the merriment begin!

"All right, everyone! Good practice!" Coach Rincon said, slapping his hands together as he pushed himself up off the ground. He had just led us all in stretching, as he had after every practice he attended, and was now off to work out with the Florida State squad. Where he got the energy to be athletic pretty much every moment of the day, I had no idea. "Good luck tonight. I want a full report next time I see you."

"Thanks, Coach," Tara said, leading us in applause.

He lifted his hand in a wave before jogging off to chat with Coach Holmes over by the bleachers. Lindsey sighed audibly as we all watched him from behind.

"Think he has a girlfriend?" she asked.

"If he does, she is one lucky girl," Sage put in.

"Maybe he has a *boy*friend. Ever think of that?" Terrell said grumpily.

"If he does, then he is one lucky guy," Sage replied in the same dreamy tone.

Everyone laughed as Terrell grumbled. I had to hand it to Sage. Sometimes she was pretty quick. I stress *sometimes*.

I leaned back on my elbows as everyone started to hoist themselves and each other up off the ground. It was a particularly gorgeous day, so we had taken the practice out to the track, where we worked out most of football season. The sky was a bright blue and there was a cool breeze in the air that swished the palm trees lazily and kept the sweat at bay. The fresh air had worked wonders on everyone's energy and we had, in fact, had one of our first solid practices of the season. The three new girls had even gotten the motions down on "Victory Now," one of our toughest cheers. Good timing, considering our first game was that night. Thus, the "good luck" from Coach Rincon.

Daniel offered me his hand and hauled me up. "Feel like pizza?" he asked.

"Actually, I feel more like jelly," I joked, shaking out my legs.

Daniel grinned. "Come on. Let's go get my car and I'll buy you a slice before the game."

Sounded good to me. Sounded pretty darn perfect. Having Daniel on the squad was finally paying off just like I imagined it would.

The crowd was just starting to break up when Coach Holmes stopped us with a bleat of her whistle. Rincon was headed for his car and Coach had rejoined the rest of us. I had hoped she would lose the whistle once pre-tryout practices were over, but she had somehow become attached to it—probably because she had learned it was a good way to wrangle the boys. They seemed to respond to it on instinct. Maybe it was a Pavlovian thing since Daniel, Terrell and Joe all played either football or soccer.

"Take a seat, everyone," she said. "Tara has something she needs to talk to you about. It'll only take a few minutes and then you'll have plenty of time to grab some dinner and get changed before you have to be back here."

I bit my tongue to keep from groaning as I sat my tired

body down again. All I wanted right then was some food and a shower. Not at the same time, of course.

"Well, it's that time of year again," Tara said, standing up as she addressed the squad. "Fundraising time."

"Whoo-hoo!" Jaimee said, earning a few laughs.

"For those of you who are new to the squad, we hold several fundraisers during basketball season to raise money for locker decorations, hallway decorations and competition season in the fall," Tara continued.

I saw Terrell, Daniel and the other guys exchange a look, clearly wondering what they had gotten themselves into. The football team never had to hold fundraisers—they got money from the district and from ticket sales at their games. The soccer team had sold light blue SDH bandannas in the fall, but hadn't worked that hard at it. And Steven's main extracurricular was the student newspaper, which was paid for by the school.

Sometimes being a cheerleader was so unfair. We had to earn our own money to keep up our traditions and pay for our competitions. All the other teams had to do was show up. Good thing we *enjoyed* fundraising, otherwise the natives might revolt.

"Now, our first fundraiser of the season is always a bake sale," Tara continued.

"A bake sale?" Joe cut in, screwing his face up in consternation. At least he was starting to change expression once in a while. "I don't do bake sales."

I glanced at Coach. Saw her jaw clench.

"We like to keep it simple," Tara said, ignoring Joe completely. "We always make a good profit and it's perfect with Christmas and Hanukkah coming up. People usually make festive cookies and stuff. And everyone wants sweets around the holidays."

"She does have a point," Steven said, looking at the guys. "It's classic supply and demand."

"That's why we do it every year," Tara said.

"Oh, right," Joe said slowly. "There were these red and green cookies last year? I must've bought a hundred."

"Whoa. It speaks more than five words at a time," Chandra said under her breath. I stifled a laugh.

"I made those!" Jaimee said to Joe, beaming.

"Good cookies," Joe said, nodding his large head.

"Good. So, anyway—"

"Uh, there's no way I'm doing a bake sale," Terrell said, raising his hand.

Tara's eyes narrowed, but she didn't look surprised. I don't think any of us were. Somehow I couldn't exactly envision Terrell in an apron, whipping up some brownies. At least not without shackles on his arms and a gun to his head.

"Are you going to give me a problem every time I try to do something?" Tara asked.

"Only when you're doing something lame," Terrell said.

"Ooooh," a few of us intoned. Daniel and the other guys laughed.

"Truluck, do you *want* to do more laps?" Coach Holmes asked, stepping forward.

"Hey. I'm always up for a run," Terrell said, standing. That, in and of itself, was a dig. He shouldn't be standing and addressing the team while the captain was standing and addressing the team. Off Coach Holmes' burning look of disdain, he raised his hands in surrender, but didn't sit back down. "I'm just sayin', why don't we do something cool?

Like that bikini car wash they had in *Bring It On?* Now *that* would make mad cash."

"Aw, yeah," Daniel said, reaching up to slap Terrell's hand. Steven and Joe both did as well. I leveled Daniel with a glare, which took him way too long to notice.

"Such boys," Phoebe said, starting to fume.

"Sorry," Daniel told me, leaning back again. He turned a particularly embarrassed shade of pink. "I just . . . sorry."

Then I laughed. I couldn't help it. Boys were *so* predictable. I didn't think a car wash was the *worst* idea, but we all knew why the guys liked the plan. Sudsy wet girls in bikinis washing hot cars? It was the theme of half the boy-centric calendars at the mall this time of year. Not to mention one seriously inappropriate Jessica Simpson video.

Which my brother had TiVoed and saved for posterity, by the way.

Tara crossed her arms over her stomach and cocked her hip, facing off with Terrell. "And, tell me, will all of you guys be wearing bikinis for this little fundraiser as well?"

I pressed my lips together as we all looked back at Terrell. She had him there. I could not imagine Daniel and the rest of them prancing around half naked and wet. Actually, I could, and it was kind of hilarious. But then my brain could imagine almost anything, most of which would never happen in real life.

"Sure," Terrell said with a shrug. "Anything it takes to bring in the green. That's how dedicated I am to this team," he said, placing a fist in his palm with mock seriousness. Tara clucked her tongue and looked away. "And besides, you know all this is gonna look *fine* in a Speedo," Terrell added, striking a bodybuilder pose.

Even Coach Holmes had to hide a laugh behind her clipboard for that one.

"Nice to know you have no problem objectifying us or yourself," Chandra said, rolling her eyes.

"Who's talking about objectifying?" Steven piped in. "The consumers are gonna be the ones giving up their cash for a substandard car wash. That's their prerogative."

"I think we should do it," Daniel said.

"What?" Chandra blurted.

"Nice boyfriend," Phoebe muttered.

"Hey!" Daniel and I said at the same time. Phoebe really was getting testy lately.

Suddenly the entire team erupted with comments and retorts. The guys argued for the car wash, while a couple of the girls went off about how it would be so much more work than a bake sale. Autumn, ever the diplomat, suggested we all take a vote, but everyone ignored her. Things were getting a little out of hand by the time Tara finally walked over to Coach, grabbed the woman's whistle right off her chest and blew.

"All right! That's enough!" Tara shouted as soon as everyone had quieted down.

"Look, all's I'm saying is, how much money are you *really* going to make at a bake sale?" Terrell said. "It doesn't *have* to be a car wash, but we should be thinking outside the box."

"Is this cheerleading practice, or an episode of *The Apprentice?*" Chandra muttered.

Tara stood on the other side of our little klatch and faced off with Terrell over our heads. If it had been any colder out, there would have been steam coming out her ears.

"Look, Truluck." Tara said his name with the very same

condescending sneer she used to use on mine. Although his she pronounced correctly. "*We* are going to do a bake sale," she said, indicating the squad with her hands. But we all knew she was talking about the girls. "If you think you have a better idea, go for it."

"You" meaning "the guys."

Terrell squinted. I could already hear the cogs in his brain working. He was going to take this challenge very seriously. There was no way he wanted to be shown up by a bunch of girls wielding boxes of Betty Crocker. "All right. Maybe I will."

"Fine," Tara said blithely.

"Fine," Terrell retorted.

Yeah. This was gonna be trouble.

• • •

"Put it in the hoop and
Score!
To!
Win!"

I ended our halftime cheer up in a chair sit, my arms in a high V, and grinned when everyone in the stands freaked out. Flashbulbs popped throughout the bleachers, everyone trying to get shots of the first-ever coed SDH cheerleading squad. Daniel's arm trembled beneath me and I felt a swoop of foreboding, but I kept my smile on until we cradled out. He caught me perfectly. Thank goodness.

"You okay?" I asked him as I popped out of his arms.

"Just nervous, I guess. Sorry," he said.

"Hey. As long as you don't drop me, we have no problem," I told him under my breath.

We all cheered with the crowd as we jogged back to the

bleachers. Daniel looked so handsome in his brand-new blue cheerleading pants and white-and-blue sweater that I just wanted to jump him and smooch him at every single moment. All the guys looked great, in fact. They were the picture of all-American boys.

"Good job," Coach told us as we huddled up. "We just need to work on sticking the landings in unison. You should always be counting in your minds, all right? ABC. Always Be Counting."

We nodded, all of us catching our breath. The boys in particular seemed to be heaving, and I wondered if it was more from nerves than from actual exertion. I felt for them. I did. Ever since the Bayside fans had first taken note of the guys on our squad, there had been all kinds of whispers and pointing. We were all waiting for someone to shout some idiotic comment and throw us off. But so far, nothing had happened.

Maybe people were more mature than I gave them credit for.

"Okay, you can all go get a drink and hang out until the team comes back," Coach told us.

Daniel grabbed my hand and pulled me toward the lobby, where some of the spectators were milling around, snacking on candy bars and sodas from the vending machines. But instead of going for a sugar fix, he nudged me over toward the trophy case and gave me a nice, long kiss.

Ah. Just what I wanted. A Daniel fix.

"Have I ever told you how unbelievable you look in your cheerleading uniform?" he said.

"Right back at ya," I replied, all butterflies.

Over his shoulder I saw a couple of Bayside girls checking Daniel out from behind. I shot them a withering look and gave him another quick kiss. Just in case they got any ideas.

"Hey! Break it up!" Tara Timothy said, pulling Daniel away from me by the back of his sweater. "No public displays of affection between teammates. It's a rule."

"Since when?" I asked.

"Since now," Tara told me. "Got a problem?"

I rolled my eyes. "No, captain, my captain," I said.

She smiled quickly and strutted away, drunk with power.

"Love her. Really," Daniel said, leaning back against the trophy case next to me. "Love her so much, I'm thinking about mounting her head on my wall."

"Ew! Daniel!" I said with a laugh. He grinned and took my hand, holding it behind our backs so no one could see. Ah, total bliss.

"Yo, Healy! You better not be telling your girlfriend all the little details of our plan," Terrell said, coming over to slap Daniel's hand.

"Plan? What plan?" I said, standing up straight.

Daniel shook his head. "Actually, I didn't even tell her we *had* a plan," he said to Terrell. "But nice job."

"What plan?" I asked again. "Wait, you guys don't already have a fundraising idea, do you?"

"Uh, yeah, we do," Terrell said cockily. "And it's gonna blow your little bake sale right out of the water."

I released Daniel's hand and crossed my arms over the SDH on my chest as the thrill of competition sparked up inside of me. Fundraising had always been a huge part of cheerleading. We had experience on our side. What did these guys know about it? If they beat us at something as fundamental as fundraising, we were never going to live it down. It would be like beating us at our own game.

This had to be a joke. There was no way they had come up with a blow-us-out-of-the-water-sized plan in the last two hours. And with zero experience. No way.

"What?" Daniel asked me.

"You don't have a plan," I said.

"Yes, we do," Daniel replied.

"Please. Tell me another one," I said, throwing a hand up at them before sauntering away. "You can't psych me out, Healy," I said over my shoulder. "I am un-psych-able."

"Hey! Don't underestimate us just because we're guys!" Daniel said. "We can fundraise with the best of 'em!"

I laughed and walked back into the gym. But in the back of my mind the seed was planted. What, if anything, did they have up their short little sweater sleeves?

• • •

The last day of school before Christmas break was mayhem. Exams were over and the teachers had about as much interest in teaching as we had in learning, so for the most part we just hung out in our classes. Mrs. O'Donaghue showed us the Jim Carrey version of *How the Grinch Stole Christmas*, claiming that it fit into our recent conversation about adapting American literature into film, and Señorita Marquez, my Spanish teacher, taught us all the words to "Feliz Navidad" and had us singing it at the top of our lungs. Even Mr. Loreng, my evil-spitter geometry teacher, wore a Santa hat and handed out candy canes, though he did give us a "just for fun" math topics quiz. Instead of answering the questions, I drew an elaborate winter scene with a snowman in the center and handed it in.

Hey, if it was just for fun . . .

Of course, the women of the cheerleading squad were giddy not just with anticipation of the holidays and the week's vacation, but with the fact that as far as we knew, the boys had never planned a fundraiser. They had mentioned nothing about it and for the past few days had held furtive, panicked-looking meetings during every water and stretching break. Coach Holmes had already left to go home for Christmas—leaving the fundraiser in Tara's capable hands—but she was going to freak when she returned and it was revealed that the guys hadn't lifted a finger to help with the bake sale and hadn't earned a dollar on their own. They were so done. So very, very done.

Is it wrong that knowing this made me happy? I mean, Daniel may have been my boyfriend, but I still relished the idea of him and his brothers in crime getting knocked down a few pegs. Show them to mess with the fundraisers extraordinaires.

By the time classes let out, everyone in the school was one Toll House cookie shy of manic. The cheerleading squad was released from classes twenty minutes early so that we could get to the lobby and set up for the bake sale. I couldn't wait to get down there. This was going to be so much fun!

I was jogging down the stairs from the front hall when I saw Daniel and Terrell, along with K. C. Lawrence and a couple of other guys from the wrestling and football teams, jostling their way into a boys' bathroom near the cafeteria. They were all whispering urgently and a couple of them had clothing on hangers folded over their forearms.

Instantly my radar went off. Something was up.

"What're you guys doing?" I blurted.

Daniel nearly jumped out of his skin.

"Nothing!" he said, backing into the room as I pursued him. "Can't come in here," he said, pointing at the little metal sign. "Boys' room."

Then he closed the door in my face and everyone inside burst out laughing. Frustration shook me from head to foot. What were they doing in there? Did it have something to do with their fundraiser? Could they have possibly pulled something off without any of us hearing word one about it? And what did K.C. and the other guys have to do with it?

Behind the thick wooden door I heard stall doors slam and a couple of raucous shouts. Something strange was afoot in the boys' bathroom. And suddenly I smelled doom.

At least that was *all* I smelled. Hanging around outside the guys' bathroom, you just never knew.

My holiday spirit somewhat dampened, I trudged to the lobby where three tables had already been set up, Christmas and Hanukkah tablecloths smoothed over their surfaces. Tara and the others were laying out the baked goods we had all stashed in Coach Holmes' office that morning. It was a seriously impressive spread. Cookies and pound cake, fudge and brownies, muffins and carrot cake, and tons of other stuff. My stomach grumbled audibly, but even the sight of all that sugar couldn't knock the dread out of me.

"What's with the puss face, puss face?" Chandra asked.

I grabbed her hand and pulled her away from the others. No need to cause mass hysteria among the team just yet. "The guys are up to something," I whispered. "And it might be something big."

"What?" she asked, her eyes wide.

"I wish I knew," I replied. "All I know is they're not in it alone. They've got K.C. and Adam Rider and a couple of other jocks involved."

"Those thumbheads? What're they gonna do? Lift weights for money?" Chandra asked.

"Not a clue," I said.

Just then the first of the teachers—some of whom didn't have last-period classes—approached the table and strolled along, checking out the goods.

"Okay, let's not worry about it now," Chandra said. "We're on."

We took our places with the rest of the squad behind the tables as a small crowd began to form. Soon bus drivers started to come in from outside, leaving their vehicles idling. A couple of the janitors joined the line and the librarians moseyed in as well. We were just starting to do a steady, leisurely business when the bell rang, and before we knew it, we were flooded with customers. The sale was a yearly tradition and had also been heavily publicized on the morning announcements and with flyers all over the halls, so everyone was ready for it. Before long Tara was hauling in the cash so quickly, she could barely keep track of the change.

"Where are they?" I asked Chandra, scanning the crowd for a glimpse of Daniel and the others. I had to shout to be heard over the din that now filled the lobby.

"Who knows? Who cares?" she replied. "All I know is

right now we're making money and they're not. That's all that matters."

"Good point," I said with a nod. Leave it to Chandra to state the obvious.

Chandra shook her hair back. "I thought so."

"Hey, miss! Miss! Can I get that last brownie with the red sprinkles?" one of the bus drivers asked me, waving a dollar in the air.

"Absolutely!" I replied.

Soon enough, I had to forget all about the boys. We were just too busy.

"Wow. This is going well," Jaimee said to me, sneaking a chocolate chip cookie from one of the plates.

Instantly Tara's hand reached in and grabbed it away from her. "No eating the profits," she said, tossing the cookie back on the plate. "You can have the leftovers. If there are any," she added in a self-congratulatory way.

For once, she deserved to pat herself on the back. The bake sale was clearly a huge success. Brownies, cookies, cakes and muffins were disappearing like bread crumbs off a park bench. I looked up and saw Mrs. Corning, my chemistry teacher, take her slice of carrot cake into the cafeteria, along with a couple of other teachers. At first I thought they were just going in there to eat, but then I saw a freshman girl wave to her friends, all excited, and they rushed into the caf as well. Soon a murmur sprouted up throughout the lobby and everyone started to trail out toward the cafeteria doors.

"What's going on?" Tara asked.

"No idea," I replied. Though I had a suspicion. A suspicion

that the guys on the squad were in the cafeteria doing . . . something. They must have sneaked past us during the deluge of customers.

"Go check it out," she said, eyeing the doors as she made change for a parent who had just purchased a half dozen cupcakes.

She didn't have to ask me twice. I was already pretty much dying of curiosity.

"I'll come!" Jaimee offered, scurrying after me.

"Me too," Chandra said.

"Fine. But the rest of you stay," Tara said. "Get back to work."

There was a definite buzz in the air as we approached the caf. I reached out and grabbed Jaimee's hand as if I needed her for support. She squeezed back. Why did I get the distinct feeling that I did not want to know what was behind those double doors?

"What do you think it is?" Chandra asked, pausing as a pair of giggling girls rushed in ahead of us. They may as well have just scored backstage passes to an Usher concert. What the heck was going on in there?

I scoffed. "Come on. How bad could it be?" With a confidence I didn't feel, I shoved open the doors.

Nothing could have prepared me for what I saw when I walked into the room. There, standing near the windows in the cafeteria, were at least twenty guys, singing Christmas carols at the top of their lungs. Daniel, Terrell, Joe and Steven were front and center and they were surrounded by a couple dozen hotties from all the various varsity sports. K.C. and Adam—the football team's kicker—were there, along with Corey Robinson and Rick Klein from the soccer team, Todd Blauschild from the cross-country team and on and on. They were all wearing suits and ties and damn did Daniel look fine in his dark blue suit. But that wasn't even the best part. The best part was that every last one of them was wearing either a Santa hat or a yarmulke to top off their outfit.

"Oh. My. God," Jaimee said slowly.

My sentiments exactly. Clutching hands, we pushed through the crowd to get to the front, just as the guys hit the final chorus of "Deck the Halls." They were all hamming it up, acting goofy, getting everyone around them to laugh. In front of them was a huge red basket that was already filled with bills and as I watched, a pair of moms who were munching on Chandra's mother's gourmet gingerbread tossed some more cash in there. Mad cash.

Meanwhile, Bethany walked slowly around the periphery of the makeshift choir, her digital video camera up and running. Wise move, saving this one for posterity. She'd probably be able to sell the copies to every girl in school for a profit.

"They recruited all the hottest guys," Jaimee said in awe.

"Except for Christopher and his merry band of manly men," I noticed.

"This is so not fair," Chandra said. "If we did this, everyone would think we were total dorks, but they do it—"

"And it's ridiculously hot," I said.

"Exactly!" Chandra and Jaimee said in unison, Chandra throwing up a hand and letting it slap down at her side.

Irritating as it was, I was still barely able to control my grin. Guys in suits, singing. It was so basic and yet so genius.

Terrell was an evil mastermind. Either that or he was destined for a life in television programming.

The song came to a close and Daniel stepped out of line to address the crowd.

"For our next number, we'd like to do a more modern classic," he said, then slowly grinned. "Please forgive me in advance."

With that he turned his back to the crowd and hit the play button on a mini-stereo. I recognized the music and saw Daniel's life flash before my eyes about two seconds before he turned around and launched into a solo of "Santa Baby."

"Oh my God," I said, cracking up along with the crowd.

"Oh no he did not," Chandra said with a guffaw.

Jaimee clung to my arm and Chandra pressed her face into my back, unable to take it anymore. I felt them both trembling against me with laughter.

"Santa baby, I want a yacht and really that's not a lot," Daniel sang. "I've been an awful good boy, Santa baby. Hurry down the chimney tonight."

He totally hammed it up, throwing out sexy glances and waggling his hips. The crowd of freshman girls in the corner squealed and screamed like he was some kind of rock star. It was all I could do to keep myself from going over there and putting my hands over their eyes. That was *my* boyfriend. Back off, ladies!

I had to hand it to him, though. The guy really knew his audience. What could be cuter than a hot athlete, dressed in a suit, singing and winking at the crowd?

Bethany spotted me in the throng and rushed over, keeping her camera poised at all times. "Your boyfriend gets the Cojones of the Year award," she said to me. "*This* is comedy."

Wow. They had even won Bethany over. Daniel had once told me he had powers beyond my understanding. Maybe that was true.

"What's with the camera?" I asked.

"Steven asked me to film it. Apparently no one in his family could believe he was actually going to sing in public," she said.

Steven asked her? *Steven* asked her? No fair! I couldn't believe Steven Schwinn had told Bethany what was going on in advance, but Daniel had, once again, managed to keep me in the dark. This was just so wrong. But to be honest, I wasn't angry this time. The surprise was just that good. I would have been *more* upset if he'd ruined it for me.

"What people will put themselves through for the blah-rah squad," Bethany said, shaking her head. "I just don't get it."

Now that she mentioned it, Steven *was* looking wan. But he was grinning and bearing it.

"Plus, I figure this'll be great ammo for blackmail later," Bethany added.

There was the girl I knew and loved!

The rest of the guys finally joined Daniel, theoretically putting him out of his solo misery, although he looked like he was having a really good time out there. He caught my eye and I shook my head at him, practically crying from laughing so hard. I had to give the kid credit. He had guts. Especially after having his manhood teased by his brother and his friends. But it was good for the squad's bank account. Several people threw money in after his routine, probably as impressed as I was by his courage.

"What the hell?"

I turned around to find Tara right behind me. "I . . . uh . . ."

I think I was still a tad flustered from Daniel's performance. Like, dizzily incoherent style flustered. Bethany, meanwhile, trained her camera on our fearless leader. Girl really did have a nose for news.

Tara Timothy, mouth agape, took it all in slowly. The crowd, the suits, the hats, the money. I could tell she was feeling a little bit queasy. And Bethany got it all on tape. Or digital chip. Whatever.

"I told you guys to check it out, not stay and enjoy the show," Tara snapped finally.

"Sorry," Jaimee told her. "We were just—"

"And get that camera outta my face," she said, slapping Bethany's viewfinder closed.

"Hey! You break, you buy!" Bethany protested.

"Bake sale," Tara said, glaring at the rest of us. *"Now."*

Hanging our heads, we followed our leader back out of the cafeteria to the tune of "The Dreidel Song." I knew I had to be loyal to my gender, but to be perfectly honest, I, like everyone else in the Sand Dune High community, wanted to stay exactly where I was. The guys had really outdone themselves.

• • •

Finally, after what seemed like forever, the guys finished up their concert and came out to snag some refreshments from the bake sale, which was winding down. Tara, of course, made them pay for whatever they took. She was giving nothing away, especially not to them.

Soon the last stragglers left school to start their December breaks and the members of the cheerleading squad were the only people left in the lobby. Somewhere in the back of the building a vacuum ran and we could hear a pair of teachers talking somewhere down the hall. The bake-sale tables were covered in crumbs, crumpled napkins and balls of discarded cellophane. The guys sat on the floor against one wall, their sleeves rolled up and their ties loosened, laughing as they went over their concert song by song. Phoebe, Chandra and I were wiping the crumbs off the third table while the rest of the squad gathered up garbage or lounged on the benches near the walls. Suddenly, Tara slapped the cover of her lock box closed and looked across the lobby at Terrell.

"So. How was your little concert?" she asked, raising her eyebrows.

"It's getting four stars from the *Weekly Catch*," Steven joked, offering his hand to be slapped by his cohorts.

"It was very lucrative," Terrell said with a laugh. "How about your little bake sale?" he asked, mimicking her tone.

"Lucrative as well," she said noncommittally.

Terrell narrowed his eyes. He toyed with a twisted piece of red cellophane with both hands. "How lucrative?" he asked.

"This should be good," Sage said.

"What?" I said.

"Watch," Phoebe told me. "Somehow this kid knows exactly how to get right under her skin."

"I mean, how much money did you make, if you had to guess?" Terrell asked with a questioning frown.

"I bet we made more money than you did," Tara shot back.

"And there it is," Chandra said.

They were right. Tara was pretty darn predictable. There was no way she was going to back down from an implied challenge, but Terrell had worked her so that in the end, *she* had suggested they strike a bet. Like I said, evil genius.

"You're on," Terrell said. He shoved himself up off the floor, tossing his suit jacket over his shoulder, hooked on one finger. He put his other hand in his pocket and strolled over to Tara, looking all *GQ*. "And I even have an idea of the terms."

"What?" Autumn asked warily, standing up from the bench behind Tara.

"Whoever loses the bet has to wash the other side's cars," Terrell said, then slowly smiled. "In bikinis."

"Ugh!" Chandra blurted. "No way. No deal."

"You're on!" Tara said, thrusting out her hand.

"Tara!" about half a dozen girls protested.

"Don't worry," Tara said through her teeth. Then, louder. "It's not like we're going to lose."

"Yeah. You keep believin' that, baby," Terrell said, shaking her hand. "So let's count."

Daniel, Steven and Joe dove into their basket of money as Tara whipped open the lock box. The air sizzled from the sudden kinetic energy.

"Wait a minute, wait a minute!" I said, throwing up my hands. "Anyone see the obvious flaw in this plan?"

"What?" Daniel asked.

"How do we know we can trust you?" I said, crossing my arms over my chest. "You could count that up and tell us you have five thousand dollars in there."

"Maybe we do," Terrell said with a smirk.

"Uh, no. Annisa's right," Chandra said, stepping forward.

"One of us will count your money and one of you will count ours. Then each counter writes down the number and it gets verified by another member of the squad. That's the only fair way."

"Damn, you girls are paranoid," Terrell said. "Fine. Who wants to count?"

"Oh! Me!" Jaimee cried, jumping up. She *was* our resident math genius.

"I don't do math," Joe said.

"I got it," Steven volunteered.

All there was to do after that was wait. Tara hovered over Steven as he counted and Terrell paced back and forth behind Jaimee, gnawing on his bottom lip. Part of me wanted to take out whatever money I had in my wallet and slip it into the lock box. I guess after watching all those people blithely toss their green at the guys' feet, I wasn't feeling all that confident.

Finally Jaimee wrote down her figure, folded the paper and held it up. No one moved. I glanced around at my friends and shrugged.

"I'll go," I offered. I was salivating to see what was on that paper anyway. How the rest of them weren't was beyond me.

"What?" I asked Jaimee, noticing her pallor as I approached.

"Just . . . take it," she said.

Never had I heard Jaimee the Peppy sound so ominous. Heart in my throat, I unfolded the scrap of paper. I couldn't believe the number when I saw it.

Seven hundred thirty-two dollars? That was ridiculous! How in the world had they made that? Quickly I ran some numbers in my head. There were only about eight hundred students in the entire *school*. But then, if only a third of the student population of the school had given them two dollars each . . . And then there were the teachers, parents, bus drivers and custodians, all of whom had more money than the kids did and could put in however much they wanted. Meanwhile, all our baked goods had fixed prices.

Gulp.

I had a feeling we were in trouble.

My mouth dry, I took the bills in hand. Meanwhile, on the other side of the room, Daniel got to work double-counting our earnings. I counted as quickly and accurately as possible, trying to get done before Daniel did. As if my being a faster counter would somehow mean something in this competition. No such luck, anyway. Out of the corner of my eye, I saw Daniel finish when I was barely even three quarters of the way through. Not a good sign. When I was done, I wrote down my figure. I had come up with the exact same number as Jaimee had.

"All set?" Tara said.

I nodded and stood up, wondering if she'd ever heard that old adage about not killing the messenger.

"Well? What do we got?" Terrell asked.

"Ladies first," Daniel said with a small smile.

I took a deep breath and looked at the scrap of paper in my hand, even though I didn't have to. I'd memorized the figure when Jaimee had first shown it to me.

"Seven hundred and thirty-two dollars," I said.

Tara choked on her own breath. Chandra whistled. Daniel laughed. He laughed. I felt my face burn. He couldn't laugh at me! That was so wrong!

"Why? What? How much did we make?" I asked.

"Three hundred and ten," Daniel said, turning the paper around so we could all see.

"Aw yeah!" Terrell cheered as the girls' side groaned. He slapped hands with all the guys and then started chanting as he danced around the lobby. "You're washing *my* car! You're washing *his* car! And oh yeah, *his* car!" he sang, pointing at each of the guys in turn.

"I don't believe this! You made more than double?" Tara shrieked.

"That's called 'no overhead,' baby!" Terrell cheered. "Best idea ever, man," he said, slapping Daniel's hand.

"Thanks, my brotha," Daniel said, bumping shoulders with him.

I just stared as my entire world was redrawn and recolored in front of my face. Preconceived notions out, reality in.

"Wait a minute. That was *your* idea?" I asked Daniel.

He smiled and shrugged innocently. I couldn't believe it. All this time, not only had he kept the plan a secret from me, but it had been *his* plan. There's no way I ever would have been able to keep my mouth shut if I had come up with something that good. I would have been all too ready to show off my brilliance.

Hey. It happens so infrequently, a girl has to give herself a chance to bask.

"Eh. I do what I can," Daniel said, all modest.

Unreal. Apparently they were *all* evil masterminds.

I walked over to join Tara and the other girls as Terrell, Daniel, Joe and Steven celebrated and chanted their new favorite song. Talk about sore winners. The longer they went on, the more I wanted to smack each one of them upside the head. Yes. Even Daniel. Although, you know, I'd probably smack him less hard.

"See? I told you they were going to screw up everything," Tara said.

"God, I hate them," Phoebe put in.

"Well, technically, they did a good thing, making all that money," Autumn said, chewing on a chunk of her white-blonde hair. "Right?"

"Less work for us," Sage said.

"True. In the long run," Felice conceded. Then, off Tara's patented look of death, she added, "Oh, but I still hate them."

Tara groaned, grabbed up the lock box and stormed off. With a sigh, we all gradually got back to cleaning up.

"Know what really sucks?" Chandra said, watching as the guys started to dance around in a little conga line.

"That?" I asked, lifting my chin toward the guys.

"Yeah, that," Chandra said as she shoved a leftover chocolate cookie into her mouth. "But also . . . now I gotta buy a bikini."

Here's the thing about Christmas Day. It is hands-down the best day of the year. Even if it is eighty degrees and humid outside. Reasons Christmas rocks? Well, 1) Giving presents. I love making other people happy. Especially my brother, who, while he normally bites the big one, always has the best reaction to gifts. 2) Getting presents. I like new swag as much as the next girl. 3) Food. You get to eat. A lot. All day long. Pancakes and sausage for breakfast. Christmas cookies for lunch. Ham and turkey and mashed potatoes for dinner. Then more cookies. It sounds disgusting, but it's actually heaven. 4) Singing all those fabulous classic Christmas songs at the top of my lungs in church. It's the one day when even the people who never sing at a single service all year get up and belt it out. 5) Christmas specials. Rudolph, Ralphie, the Grinch, George Bailey, Olive the Other Reindeer. Perfect vegging material. Especially when you're in a food coma. (See No. 3.)

I love every minute of it. And this year, it was going to be especially perfect.

Because this year I had a boyfriend. A boyfriend who was coming over after his family returned from his grandparents' in Boca so that we could exchange gifts. That's right,

I got to top off the best day ever with a visit from Daniel Healy.

"Ugh! I'm never eating again," Gabe announced, appearing in the living room doorway after finishing his third helping of dinner. He slumped against the door frame, looking ruddy and dazed. I could hear the sounds of whooshing water and clanking dishes coming from the kitchen as my parents cleaned up. This was the one day all year they didn't make us help out. (That should probably be No. 6 on the list.) Maybe they apologized to each other for all the decoration switching over a sink full of sudsy pots and pans.

"What happened? Did you hit table?" I asked.

"You're a real comedian, you know that?" Gabe replied. "What're we watching?"

"*White Christmas,*" I said, my foot tapping nervously against the floor. I just wanted Daniel to get there already. I wanted to give him his present and see his reaction. And, of course, I was *dying* to see this big surprise gift he had for me.

Unable to lounge around the table with the family over coffee and pie, I had long since bailed to coif for my romantic get-together. (Apparently anticipation of a boyfriendly encounter negates the food coma.) Once I finished applying my new shimmery lip balm (stocking stuffer), I retreated to the living room to sit by the tree, watch Christmas movies and try to stop looking at my watch. I kept giving myself challenges.

Okay, when they're done singing "Snow," I can check my watch. . . . Okay, the next time the skinny chick shows her legs, I can check my watch. . . .

"Oh . . . yeah," Gabe groaned, dropping down next to me on the couch and unfastening his leather belt. He lifted his T-shirt and patted his tummy. I heard a distinct gurgle. "That's what I'm talkin' about."

I checked my watch. Two minutes until Daniel was supposed to get here.

"Ew, freakshow. Do I want to see your gut right now?" I said, shoving his leg before he could put it up on my lap.

"I have a gut?" Gabe cried, looking down at his flat stomach.

"Made you look!" I teased.

Gabe rolled his eyes and sat back. "Very mature."

"Hey, it's Christmas," I said, lifting my shoulders with a grin.

Gabe looked me up and down and shifted over slightly so he could see me better. "What's with the skirt? And why are you so perky?"

At that moment the doorbell rang and I jumped up. Daniel was one minute early. "I got it!" I cried.

I ran for the door and whipped it open. Daniel stood on the doorstep in a green V-neck sweater with a white T-shirt under it, his hair shiny with product for the occasion. He held a small red package in both hands. Holy heart palpitations.

"Merry Christmas, Jersey," he said with a grin.

If someone could package *that* and sell it this time of year, they could make a fortune. I threw my arms around his neck and gave him a big, fat kiss. Daniel almost fell backward in surprise.

"Sorry," I said, giggling. "I've been wanting to do that all day."

"Me too," he said. "Nanny and Pop Pop's is cool and all, but it's a lot less interesting when you've got Annisa Gobrowski waiting for you at home."

Oh. My. God. Had he been planning that speech all the way up here? And wait, who cared? He kissed me again and I almost melted.

"Annisa! Who was at the door?" my father called.

I sprang away from Daniel and hauled him inside. "It's just Daniel! We're gonna open our presents!"

"Okay! Tell him to come in for some dessert when you're done!" my mother called out.

"Thanks, Mrs. G!" Daniel shouted back.

We walked into the living room, where Gabe was now sprawled out on the couch, his hand still covering his bare stomach. He had switched the TV over to *A Christmas Story.*

"Gabe!" I said through my teeth.

Gabe slid his eyes toward us without moving his head. "Hey, man," he said. "Wh'sup?"

"Hey," Daniel replied warily. Not that I could blame him. The last time he'd seen Gabe, the guy had been all Calvin Klein-ed out. "Uh . . . I think you have some mashed potato in your 'stache."

I narrowed my eyes. Sure enough, there was a white blob on the edge of Gabe's facial fuzz. Where was a good death ray when you needed one?

"Really?" Gabe said. He touched his fingers to his mustache, then licked them. Licked them! Why not just tell Daniel we were both raised in a barnyard?

"That your bike out there, man?" Daniel asked.

"Yeah. Sweet, isn't it?" Gabe asked. "Wanna go for a spin?"

"Oh, thanks, but no way," Daniel said. "Those things are death traps."

"Ha! He gets double dessert!" my father shouted from the kitchen.

"Thanks a lot, dude," Gabe said derisively.

"Gabe, do you think you could give us a few minutes?" I asked.

"Why do you get the living room?" he asked, propping himself up, with some effort, onto his elbows.

Uh, because you're disgusting and embarrassing and should be locked up behind closed doors somewhere, reading Emily Post?

"Because we want to open our presents by the tree," I said.

He let out a loud belch. God, I missed the metrosexual Gabe. He never would have let his bodily functions run amok like this.

"Presents?" Gabe pushed himself up and squared off with Daniel. His T-shirt finally fell down to cover his pale skin, thank God. "What'd you get my sister, dude? That better not be a ring."

Daniel's face nearly burned right off. Which would have been a tragedy of Shakespearian proportions.

"Gabe! Just get out already!" I demanded.

Gabe narrowed his eyes at Daniel before ever so slowly backing toward the door. "I'm watching you, man," he said. He made a V with his fingers and pointed them from his eyes to Daniel's. That was when I had to shove him out of the room. He almost toppled the sideboard in the hallway, but it was totally worth it.

"Ooof!" Gabe shouted.

"What was that?" my mother called.

"I'm all right! We're all good!" Gabe said before finally, *finally* stumbling for the stairs.

"So! Where were we?" I said, turning to Daniel.

"Is he gonna be okay?" Daniel asked.

I waved my hand toward the hallway. "Don't worry about him. Bikers have thick skins." I picked up Daniel's present from under the tree and sat down on the couch, pulling my feet up under me. Daniel cleared his throat and sat down as well, adjusting the pillows behind him. In the dim glow of the Christmas tree he was even more handsome than ever. My heart fluttered at his nearness. This was already the best Christmas ever.

"So? Who goes first?" I asked.

"Let me," Daniel said. "I actually have two things for you to open."

Two things? Two things? But I only got him one!

"Don't worry. It's nothing big," Daniel said, seeing my pallor. He pulled an envelope out of his back pocket and handed it over. *Crap. A card? I didn't get him a card!* "Go ahead," he said.

My excitement slightly rocked by guilt, I slipped my finger under the flap and opened the envelope. A small piece of paper fluttered out into my lap.

It was a handmade coupon—one free "get out of bikini car-washing" pass.

"Oh, very funny," I said, whacking Daniel's shoulder.

"You like it?" he asked with glee.

He was gloating. That much was obvious. The little jerk.

But I was willing to let it go because it was, you know, Christmas. Plus, he was my boyfriend. The operative syllable being "boy." Even the perfect ones can be jerks sometimes.

"I love it," I said sarcastically, holding it to my heart. "I never wanted anything more."

Daniel snickered, pleased with himself.

"But I can't accept it," I said. "I was part of the bet. I have to keep up my end."

Daniel tilted his head. "All right, but I should warn you. Terrell and Joe are planning on going off-roading next weekend."

Jerks, the little devil on my shoulder said.

But I grinned beatifically. "No problem whatsoever." I held his present out to him. "Your turn."

That second present better not be a joke gift too, or I can't be responsible for my actions, I thought.

Daniel smiled and turned the package over. He started with the ribbon, actually untying the knot with his short fingernails. Then he removed it slowly and placed it on the couch next to him before examining the paper, like he was looking for the best way in.

Just rip it! I thought. *Come on, man! It's Christmas!*

Daniel smiled up at me and I erased the consternation from my face. He popped the tape off with his finger and unfolded the wrapping paper.

How does he do *this?* I wondered. Present unwrapping at the Healy house must have taken hours. I was amazed that they had time to drive to Boca and back.

Finally, *finally,* Daniel got to the last piece of tape. "Holy . . . I can't believe you did this!" Daniel said, turning the box of CDs over in his hands. "This is too much."

"Eh, I got a good deal," I said, giddy. "You like it?"

"Like it? I love it," he said, reaching over and giving me a hug. "I can't wait to listen to these."

"We can put one in right now!" I suggested, standing up.

"Wait, wait, wait!" Daniel said, reaching for my arm. "Don't you want your present first?"

Oh, right. I had forgotten about that. Sort of. Okay, not at all.

"Here. Sit," Daniel said.

I did, and he handed the small box over. My face was warm with pleasure as I imagined what might be inside. For a split second. Then I tore into it like a doggie on a beef bone.

"Wow. You really don't waste any time," Daniel said.

"Nuh-uh," I told him, tossing the shredded paper aside. I lifted the lid off the box and there, sitting against a white cotton square, was a silver charm bracelet with a single heart charm. My own heart gave an extra-hard thump.

"Daniel! It's beautiful!" I said.

"Check it out," he said, sliding closer to me. He lifted the bracelet out of the box and into the light. I squinted and saw that on one side of the heart, my initials had been engraved in a swirly script, AG. Daniel turned the delicate heart over, revealing his initials on the other side, DH.

"Oh! That's so sweet! I love it!" I said, tears prickling at my eyes.

Daniel smiled. "Wanna put it on?"

"Definitely," I said, holding out my arm.

It took Daniel a couple of tries, but eventually he worked the tiny clasp and attached the cool silver to my wrist.

"I'll wear it every day," I said, admiring the bracelet against the light of the tree.

Daniel blushed. "You don't have to do that."

"No! I want to. It's beautiful. I love it," I said.

"I love you," Daniel replied.

Instantly the world stopped spinning. All the furniture in the room fell over and the Christmas tree crashed to the ground. All I could hear was the kids on the TV taunting, "You'll shoot your eye out! You'll shoot your eye out!"

"You . . . wh . . . what?" I said.

Daniel looked me in the eye. His expression was super-intensely serious. He whispered, "I love you, Annisa."

Slowly a smile spread its way across my face. Daniel smiled back. "I love you too," I said.

Christmas totally rocks.

"All right, everyone, hands in," Coach Holmes called out.

It was Wednesday night of our winter break and we were in the middle of the annual district holiday tournament, being held at our rival school, West Wind High. Eight teams from the district were competing in the tournament and it was just the first round.

We all gathered into a huddle, all twenty of us plus Coaches Holmes and Rincon, who had driven up to watch us in action. Everyone put their hands together in the center of the circle. At halftime, our team was down by fifteen points against Clearwater High. But even so, our little circle was infused with electricity. This was it. Our entire athletic division was about to see us in action for the first time.

My bare arm rubbed up against Daniel's and I had to steel myself to keep a visible shiver from running down my side. He grinned quickly at me, knowing exactly how I felt. Ever since we'd said "I love you" to each other, we hadn't been able to stop saying it, and every time he so much as brushed my hand with his, I felt everything inside of me sizzle.

"Gobrowski! You with me?" Coach Holmes asked.

Snagged!

"Yes, Coach," I said firmly, prickling with embarrassment under my uniform.

"Good. Now this is our first time trying this cheer at a game," she said, looking around at each of us. "I want you to visualize those stunts, especially that throw," she said, staring right at me. I gulped. We had only executed the basket toss with layout once successfully. Once. "Confidence, poise, safety. Got me?"

We all nodded. I had never seen everyone look so determined. Guess that was what happened when every cheerleader from all the local schools was there to watch us soar or crash.

Soar. Definitely soar.

"Good. Now get out there and let's show these people what we can do," she said. "On three. One, two, three!"

"Whaddup, Sand *Dune!*" we all shouted, throwing our arms in the air.

The Sand Dune High section of the crowd went wild as we took the floor. I jogged into position, my heart pounding erratically, and caught a glimpse of the West Wind High cheerleaders gathered near the door. They all had serious pusses on as they eyed us and talked to each other behind their hands. Jealous much, ladies? Well, they were going to be a lot more jealous in a minute when they saw the extension of my elevation.

Aw, yeah!

" 'Win, Win, Win!' Ready?" Tara shouted.

"Okay!

Come on! Yellow and blue! Win! Win! Win!

Come on! Yellow and blue! Win! Win! Win!"

We shifted formation and the girls at the front grabbed

their signs from the floor. I took my position at the center of the squad with Daniel, Terrell and Joe around me.

You can do this, Annisa. Don't get scared, now. Show those West Wind girls what you've got.

"Come on! Sand Dune fans! All join in!

Come on! Sand Dune fans! Win! Win! *Win!*"

Chandra, Autumn and Tara thrust their signs into the air one at a time and the crowd responded louder and louder with each successive "Win!"

"Come on! Sand Dune fans! Win! Win! *Win!*"

"Once more!" Tara shouted.

"Here we go," Daniel said under his breath.

On the count I popped up onto his and Terrell's hands. I stayed tight and concentrated, staring straight ahead.

Down, up, over, down. Down, up, over, down. Down, up, over—

"Come on! Sand Dune fans! Win!"

Down, up!

"Win! Win!"

And I flew into the air higher than I'd ever flown before. I heard the crowd gasp and wanted to close my eyes, thinking something was wrong. But instead, I executed my layout, thrust my arms out at my sides and hoped for the best as I plummeted toward the ground.

Just don't crack open your skull. You need *your skull,* I heard a little voice whisper.

And the next second I was safe in Daniel's, Terrell's and Joe's arms. My eyes opened in surprise and it was the first moment I realized I *had* closed them. Oops! They popped me to my feet and I could feel the glee and relief radiating off the guys as we all thrust our arms into the air and ran back to the stands. Coach Holmes was beside herself, applauding and shaking her head as she laughed. The whole crowd was on its feet, even the fans from other schools.

"That was sweet!" Terrell said, slapping my hand as he sat down behind me.

"No doubt," I said.

As we sat, we all saw the West Wind girls filing out into their lobby. They looked like they'd just been through electroshock group therapy, and their green complexions matched their uniforms. Oh yeah. Bringing guys onto the squad was a good idea. I no longer cared what Tara or anyone else said. The looks on those girls' faces made it all worth it.

• • •

When we walked into the gym on our first Monday back, Coach Holmes and Coach Rincon were sitting on the bottom bleacher, turned toward each other, their knees practically touching. Autumn stopped in her tracks and I nearly slammed right into her.

"What?" I said.

"Shhh!" She backed me out of the gym as Chandra, Tara and a few other girls came up behind us. "There's a total love vibe in the air in there."

"Huh?" Tara said as we gathered around the windows.

Coach Holmes giggled and shoved Coach Rincon's shoulder backward. He reached out and touched her face with his hand. Holy inappropriateness. They were staring into each other's eyes. Gazing, actually.

"Omigod. Did she just *giggle*?" Chandra said.

"Are they gonna *kiss*?" Tara asked.

The guys came up behind us and I knew there was no way we could let them see this. They already gave Coach Holmes enough crap. This would send them into spasms. I yanked the door open and practically shouted over my shoulder.

"Aren't you guys *so* psyched to be back?"

My maneuver had the desired effect. The coaches sprang apart and stood up. Coach Holmes cleared her throat and Rincon took a deep breath, smoothing down the front of his shirt.

"Hello, everyone!" Coach Holmes called out, clutching her clipboard for dear life. "Welcome back!"

"How was *your* break?" Autumn asked pointedly, looking from one coach to the other.

"It was fine, Autumn, thanks for asking," Coach Holmes said, just as pointedly. Whether or not she knew we'd seen them was unclear, but she obviously wanted to get on with business. "Now if you'll all have a seat . . ."

Soon everyone was gathered in the bleachers. I couldn't stop staring at Coach Rincon, who couldn't stop staring at his feet. What was going on between these two?

"All right! All right, everyone! Let's calm down!" Coach Holmes called out. "I know you're all excited to be back—"

Major groans from the peanut gallery, followed by a few laughs.

"But now that all the dust has settled from the holidays, we have a few things to discuss," Coach continued.

I saw Tara glance warily at Phoebe and wondered if they knew something I didn't know. Who was I kidding? They almost always knew something I didn't know. Behind Chandra's back, Daniel reached over and hooked his pinky

117

around mine. My new bracelet dangled between our legs as we smiled.

We were so gross, *I* could almost gag. Almost.

Of course I would have to take the bracelet off before we started practice. No jewelry allowed, especially when stunting. But I was waiting until the very last second.

I wondered if Coach Rincon had given Coach Holmes anything romantic over the holidays. I watched them closely, trying to imagine them holding pinkies or saying "I love you." They definitely would have made a seriously hot couple.

"First of all, great job at the holiday tournament!" Coach Holmes said enthusiastically.

"Yeah!" Coach Rincon added, clapping his hands.

We all joined in, happily. There was clearly a lot of pride in the room. Along with that lingering love vibe.

"Even though we only got to cheer one game before our team was eliminated—"

Grumbles all around.

"It was one kickass game for us," Coach continued.

"You better believe dat!" Terrell said. Everyone laughed and clapped some more.

Coach Holmes held her hands up to quiet us down. "Now I also want to congratulate all of you on a job well done with the holiday fundraisers," she continued, consulting her clipboard as we cheered some more, though this time the guys outshouted the girls. "From what I see here, you brought in a total of one thousand forty-two dollars."

"And earned ourselves some free car washes," Terrell said, knocking fists with Joe and Steven.

"Good job. Really. I'm proud of you," Coach said, hugging her clipboard. "I just wish you had all found a way to work *together* to earn this money."

Silence fell. Tara looked at Phoebe again. So she *did* know something negative was coming. Coach walked up and down the bleachers, surveying us.

"It seems that we have a misunderstanding on our hands," she said. "This is one team. Not a girls' team and a boys' team, but one cohesive team."

"You should be working *with* each other, not against each other," Rincon added sternly.

Terrell leaned back on his elbows and jutted his chin out. I knew he was taking this lecture as a personal attack on him. And I didn't blame him. It *had* been his idea to do a second fundraiser.

"I'll admit that this time your competitive natures benefited the team," Coach Holmes continued. "But if this continues, it's only going to act as a poison as the season goes on, so I want to nip it in the bud. I want you guys to start figuring out some ways to bond. Figure out a way to become the solid unit I want you to be."

No one moved. If someone had dropped a Q-Tip in the locker room on the other side of the gym, I think we would have heard it. It wasn't like I didn't want to be one cohesive team with the guys. I did. And I'm sure everyone else wanted that too. But why was she saying this to us now? We had done our job at the tournament perfectly. We were all on a natural high. So why was she bringing us down? Wasn't cheering all the other squads in the district into submission enough for her?

"Any suggestions?" Coach said finally, raising her perfectly plucked brows. "Ideas for group activities."

Jaimee sat forward and raised her hand, tossing her long, bouncy blonde ponytail over her shoulder. "I know!"

"Yes, Jaimee?" Coach Holmes said, letting out a relieved breath.

"We have the first big rivalry games against West Wind next week, right?" she said, looking around. "So we're gonna need to decorate the seniors' lockers and make banners and bake—"

"I don't think I like where this is going," Terrell said quietly, earning a laugh from his male counterparts. Tara clucked her tongue and rolled her eyes.

"So how about we have a craft party this weekend?" Jaimee suggested, earning a guffaw from Terrell. Her cheeks turned pink, but she soldiered on. "We can do it at my house on Saturday night. I'm sure my parents won't mind."

Rincon snorted a laugh. You could have knocked everyone over with a feather. Coach Holmes shot him a look of death and he quickly covered his mouth with his hand and tried to adopt a serious expression. Unfortunately, however, the damage was done.

"What?" Jaimee said uneasily.

"Nothing. That sounds like a perfect idea," Coach Holmes said, forcing a smile. "Thank you, Jaimee."

"Uh, a craft party? No, thanks," Terrell said, lifting his foot to rest on his knee.

"I don't do crafts," Joe added.

"You do now," Tara said flatly.

Daniel tipped his head back and groaned. Apparently the idea of a night of glue and glitter didn't please him either.

"Come on, you guys, don't think of it as a craft party," I

said, turning in my seat so I could see the boys better. "We'll get junk food, we'll hang out, we'll—"

"Cut out letters and crabs and little basketballs," Steven finished, none too enthused.

Suddenly everyone was arguing again. Just like that, the boys vs. girls line had been redrawn. Coach Holmes finally had to blow her whistle to get us to shut up.

"Listen up! Decorating for rivalry games is a big part of being on this squad," Coach Holmes said. "You all will be there and you all will—"

"Come on, Dee. You're really gonna make them *craft*?" Coach Rincon said.

An anvil dropped out of the sky and flattened his head. Or it might as well have. Ever so slowly, Coach Holmes turned to face Coach Rincon. The vein must've been visible from space.

"Coach Rincon? Will you excuse me while I run my team?" she said through her teeth.

His arms dropped to his sides and his nostrils flared as he stared at her. "Your team," he said.

"Yes. *My* team," she replied.

"All right then. I think I'll just go get some water," he replied. "Why don't you come and get me when *you're* ready."

"Thanks, I think I will," Coach Holmes said.

Rincon shook his head with a wry smile, turned and sauntered out. Huh. Was this a trouble-in-paradise moment?

"Man's right," Terrell said as soon as Rincon was gone, agreeing with the guy for the first time ever. "The guys shouldn't have to go participate. We'd probably suck at it anyway."

Coach Holmes rolled her eyes to the ceiling and shook her head, at a loss for words. None of us had ever seen her at a loss for words before and my heart went out to her. It had to have something to do with the snipes between her and Rincon. It was amazing how spying one intimate moment changed the interpretation of everything.

"You're going to be there," Tara said.

"No. We're—"

"Hey! You guys are gonna be there, and you're gonna like it!" Tara said, standing and turning on them.

Terrell looked up at her slowly and for a split second, I thought they were going to finally throw down. Tara's eyes narrowed further and further as Terrell's nostrils flared. I imagined them flying up into the air and then grabbing each other's necks, *Matrix* style.

Now that was a fight I'd like to see. The PG version, of course. My money would be on Tara. Terrell was strong, but Tara was vicious. She'd scratch his eyes right out of his head if provoked.

"Fine," Daniel said finally, glancing warily in Coach Holmes' direction. "We'll be there."

"Gee. I can't wait," Terrell said sarcastically. "Can we practice now? Sage and I have a cupie to perfect."

The cupie, a stunt in which the flyer stands with both feet on her base's hand, was the hardest stunt we had learned yet. And none of us had mastered it. Terrell really knew how to change a subject. He was aware that Coach Holmes was dying to show our cupies off at the West Wind game.

"Sounds like a plan to me," Coach said, and blew her whistle. "Hit the mats!"

Terrell grinned triumphantly and jumped to the gym floor. Once more the cheer crisis of the century was averted.

• • •

Coach Rincon did come back and he did help all of us perfect our cupies, but there was clearly tension in the air between him and Coach Holmes. Finally, on one of our take-fives, they walked out of the gym together and up the stairs to the athletic department offices. We all watched them go with badly disguised interest.

"What do you think they're doing up there?" Autumn asked as we walked ever so slowly toward the water fountain.

"I think Coach is tearing him a new one," Phoebe said.

"You know, your imagery has gotten really violent lately," Autumn told her. "Is everything okay?"

"Never better," Phoebe said flatly, then turned and shoved her way through the doors.

"College applications," Tara explained to the rest of us. "You'll understand when you're seniors."

I had a feeling that it was also Phoebe's parents' divorce, her part-time job and keeping up with school, cheerleading and stunting that was getting to her. Every day it seemed like the girl was one step closer to snapping.

"Let's go listen in," Sage suggested, looking hungrily at the door to the office.

"No! You can't do that," I said, even though I was practically salivating to know what was going on.

"Yes, I can," Sage said with a mischievous grin. "And you're going with me."

She grabbed my arm and dragged me toward the door that led to the offices. I couldn't have been more shocked if she'd pulled me by the hair.

"Why me?" I asked, yanking my arm away.

"Because! She *loves* you," Sage said, as if it were the most obvious thing in the world. "If she catches us, she'll go easy on us. If she caught me alone, she'd kill me."

There was Sage logic for you. But I let her drag me along with only one helpless glance over my shoulder at Daniel and the rest of my teammates. They looked understandably baffled. After all, since when did Sage and I do anything together other than fight? But I was too intrigued to turn back. I'm not proud of it, but I was. Some dirt is just too juicy.

Ew.

Clutching hands—spying brings people together, apparently—Sage and I tiptoed up the steps and around the corner. Coach Holmes' office was the second door on the left, and she had left it slightly ajar. Already, the two of them were yelling at each other. Sage and I ducked back around the corner and huddled there, listening.

"—you call me Dee in front of my squad?"

"I'm sorry, but what's with all this 'my squad, my squad'?" Coach Rincon retorted. "I thought I was a coach here too."

"Yeah, a guest coach," she replied. "What were you thinking, contradicting me in front of the team?"

"I'm sorry for that, okay? But Deirdre, come on. Making the guys do signs and banners and stuff? That's torture," he said.

"You're overstating the situation a bit, aren't you, Leo?" she replied. "I'm not suggesting we electrocute them or something. Besides, this is part of what this team does."

"Well, it's just stupid," he replied.

Sage and I looked at each other, wide-eyed. Had he never seen Coach Holmes go nuclear? 'Cause he was about to.

"You're telling me that if we had to make banners back at school, you wouldn't have participated?" she said. "Mr. Team Team Team would have, what, quit?"

"No. I don't know," he said, clearly frustrated. "I guess it's a good thing we never had to find out."

"Oh, that's just great," she said.

"Look, I just don't think it's fair, that's all," Rincon said.

"Fine. Think whatever you want. But from now on, keep those thoughts to yourself," she said.

"Real nice, Dee," Rincon spat back. "Is this what our marriage is gonna be like too?"

Sage bleated in surprise and we both slapped our hands over our mouths. Then we both turned and tore down the stairs, shoving each other all the way to try to get ahead of each other. Just before the door slammed behind us, I heard the two coaches were still shouting. Apparently, they hadn't heard us. Though how that was possible, I had no idea.

"They're getting *married*?" Sage cried the moment we hit the floor of the now deserted gym.

"They're getting married," I repeated, dumbstruck.

"Omigod, I have to tell everyone," Sage said.

"Not if I tell them first!" I shouted. And once again, the race was on.

"Felice, could you pass me the glitter glue?" Daniel asked, holding his hand out over the crafting table in Jaimee's rec room on Saturday night. Everyone stopped what they were doing and looked at him. Daniel blanched. "Did I just say pass me the glitter glue?" he said. "Oh, God."

"I think you just officially became a girl," Tara joked, looking at him over an elaborate blue crab she was cutting out of poster board.

"Yeah. Good thing your brother wasn't here to hear you say that," Terrell called from across the room. "He'd be calling an exorcist right about now."

Felice tossed him the glue from the other end of the table. Daniel caught it in one hand and placed it down on the newspaper that protected the wood surface of the furniture, looking nauseated. Outside, the waves of the ocean crashed. Jaimee's family was apparently seriously loaded. Three of the four walls of her house looked out over the ocean and the whole place was floor-to-ceiling windows. Even the rec room on the bottom floor had a gorgeous view, considering it was reserved for her brother's playdates, her grandmother's senior club gatherings and Jaimee's craft nights.

"It's gonna be okay," I said, patting him on the back. "No

one's revoking your man status." I lowered my voice and glanced across the room, where Terrell and Joe were playing on Jaimee's brother's Xbox 360, screaming and yelling at the big-screen TV as they decimated some desert enemy. "Real men work with their team instead of ignoring our existence all night long."

"Girl has a point," Chandra said, gluing a yellow SDH megaphone down on a white background. "Besides, there's nothing sexier than a guy who knows how to use glitter glue. Right, Annisa?"

"Oh, totally."

Daniel looked down at the yellow star he had cut out, which he was about to outline with the glitter glue. He placed the star in front of me and pulled a piece of orange paper toward him.

"Thanks, but I think I'll just cut out the circles for the basketballs for now," he said with a wan smile.

Chandra and I laughed. "Good plan."

I smiled to myself as I got back to cutting and decorating stars. So far craft night had been fairly successful. Shira, Wendy and Ally, the new team members, had been in charge of snacks and had gone all-out, bringing everything from a veggie-and-dip platter to boxes of Twinkies and Oreos. All the girls were sitting at the various card tables Jaimee's grandmother had collected for the train dominoes game she hosted each week, making decorations for the seniors' lockers. Upstairs, Kimberly, Autumn, Maureen and Michelle baked cookies and brownies to be boxed up and stashed in the lockers as well. And even though Terrell and Joe had done nothing but play video games since they had arrived, at least Daniel was helping. As was Steven, who was laid out on the floor with Jaimee, painting a banner for the front lobby.

"This is gonna be the best banner ever," Jaimee said, admiring her design with pride. The slogan read "Snag the Dolphins" and at the end was a drawing of a mean-looking crab holding a dolphin up in its pincers over its head.

"You *are* an artiste," Steven said as he filled in one of the letters with blue paint.

Jaimee beamed with pride. There wasn't much she loved more than craft parties. Unless it was getting complimented on her hard work.

Lindsey walked by in her high-heeled boots, stepping carefully around the banner as she balanced two cups of soda. Her curly blonde hair was pulled back from her face with tendrils grazing her cheeks and she was wearing super-tight jeans and a cleavage-baring top, while the rest of us had rolled in wearing sweats and T-shirts.

"Hey, Lindsey! What do you think of my sign?" Jaimee asked.

Lindsey barely glanced at it. "It's great," she said blithely. Then she placed one of the soda cups in front of Joe and stepped up next to the TV, jutting her hip into his line of vision.

"I got you a soda," she said hopefully. "If you want to pause it."

"I don't do breaks," Joe said.

Karianna, who was sitting on the couch next to Joe—well, practically in Joe's lap—smirked. Lindsey's expression darkened, but she wasn't about to give up. "Who's winning?" she asked.

"Joe is," Karianna said, hooking her arm around Joe's on the couch and looking at him like he was the love of her life.

"Please! Terrell is kicking his ass," Sage said. She was perched on the arm of the couch right next to Terrell, her butt practically up in his face.

Did I say the girls were all helping with the crafts? I lied. Certain girls had no interest in helping anyone but themselves.

"So annoying," Phoebe said under her breath as she finished cutting out the last of her letters. She looked over her shoulder as Sage cheered some victory of Terrell's. "We're doing all this work and on Monday they're gonna get just as much credit as we are for being here."

"Not if I have anything to say about it," Tara said.

I felt a quick thump of foreboding. "You're going to tell on them?"

"Why not? Phoebe's right. They shouldn't be able to take credit for our work," Tara said.

"I thought there was no I in team," Daniel said.

Over in the corner, all five of the video-gamers cheered and high-fived. Joe pulled Karianna onto his lap and Lindsey wrapped her arms around his neck from behind. Pretty soon they were all engaged in a wrestling/tickle match, arms and legs flailing everywhere. Shrieks of delight filled the room and probably brought some confused dolphins to shore outside.

"Yeah," Tara said, rolling her eyes. "Tell that to them."

"Well, maybe you should pick your battles," I suggested. "Coach Holmes is already pretty upset about this whole boys-and-craft-night thing."

"True," Chandra said. "I still can't believe Holmes and Rincon are getting *married*."

"*If* they're still getting married," Tara said under her breath.

"Come on, they're not gonna break up over one little fight," Jaimee said from the floor.

"Over a high-school cheerleading squad," Steven put in.

"I don't know, you guys," I said. "It sounded deeper than that."

"Well, it's not my responsibility to keep Holmes' engagement together," Tara said blithely. "But it is my responsibility to run this squad."

As you are constantly reminding us, I thought.

"And I'm going to talk to her," Tara added.

"Great," Daniel said sarcastically.

Yeah. Really great.

"All done!" Jaimee announced. "We just have to let it dry. What do you guys think?"

We all pushed up out of our chairs for a better look as Felice whistled, impressed. "It's awesome, James," she said.

"Totally. It *is* the best banner ever," I said.

"Yeah, it was all me," Steven said, stretching his arms above his head. Jaimee smacked him on the chest and he coughed. "Ow! Damn, girl. Violence is not the answer," he said, rubbing at his ribs.

"Sorry," Jaimee said sweetly. "It was a reflect."

"I think you mean *reflex*," Felice corrected. Then instantly slapped her own hand over her mouth.

Everyone held their breath. Felice was constantly correcting Jaimee on her misspoken words and Jaimee *hated* it. Lately Felice had been better about it, biting her tongue most of the time, but apparently this one had slipped out. I braced myself for Jaimee's oncoming breakdown.

"You're probably right," Jaimee said with a shrug. "I think I'll go check on the girls upstairs."

She grinned with pride as she pushed herself up off the floor. Felice sighed in relief. Apparently Jaimee was in too good a mood over her artistry to let little things get to her. I watched her bound up the stairs, her blonde ponytail bouncing. When Jaimee was psyched up, her attitude was infectious, and now everyone at the table was smiling instead of throwing death-ray glares at the flirtatious five.

At least one good thing had come out of tonight.

• • •

An hour later, we were just getting cleaned up when the doorbell rang, singing a soothing tune that echoed throughout the house. Terrell jumped up from the sofa, leaving behind a distinct imprint of his butt cheeks. That's what happens when you sit in the same exact position for four hours.

"That's the pizza and wings!" he announced.

Tara dropped what she was doing. "You ordered pizza and wings? The two tons of food we had wasn't enough for you?"

"Chicken feed," Terrell threw over his shoulder.

"I don't do crudités," Joe added.

"Well, whatever," Tara said, shoving scraps of paper into a garbage bag so violently, I had a feeling she was imagining shoving them down Terrell's throat. "The squad isn't paying for it."

Terrell fished his wallet out of his back pocket. "I didn't ask you to," he said. "God, Timothy. Who knew you were such a hard-ass?"

I did! I thought. As did, most likely, the rest of the team, all of whom spontaneously averted their eyes from Tara.

Terrell took the stairs two at a time and came back down a couple minutes later with two pies and a white paper bag rolled up on top of them. He obliviously placed the pies down on a table that Felice and Kimberly were trying to clean, and picked up the bag of wings.

"Yo, Healy! Think fast!" he shouted.

We all watched as the bag tumbled end over end through the air toward Daniel. He dropped the markers he had been gathering in his arms and his eyes widened. He reached for the bag, but it was over his head and out of his grasp. My breath caught in my throat as the bag opened up over our heads and splattered to the floor—right in the center of Jaimee's banner. Wings and barbecue sauce exploded everywhere, covering the crab and dolphin and shedding droplets all over Steven's carefully filled-in letters.

Total banner carnage.

"Nooooooo!" Jaimee wailed, dropping to her knees next to the mess.

She tried to pick a couple of wings up off the paper, but they left behind huge orangey-brown smears. Her work was completely ruined. For a long moment no one said a word. And then the guys, all of them, cracked up laughing.

"Daniel!" I blurted, smacking his arm with the back of my hand.

"What? I'm sorry!" he cried, putting his hand over his mouth. His eyes, however, were full of mirth.

"Jaimee? Are you all right?" Felice asked.

Jaimee slowly raised her head. Her face was covered with pink blotches. She took one look at Terrell, who was

132

doubled over, then burst into tears and ran up the stairs. Her exit only made the guys laugh harder. It's really unbelievable what guys can find funny. Did they not notice that every female in the room was glaring at them?

"What the hell is wrong with you people?" I shouted.

"Uh-oh. Tantrum!" Terrell said, loving every minute of it.

"No. No tantrums. I don't *do* tantrums," I said, glaring pointedly at Joe. "I just want to know how, exactly, you people manage to walk around without a shred of a conscience. She worked her butt off on that banner all night long and you just ruined it and then laughed in her face about it. How would you feel if that was you?"

The guys slowly stopped laughing, but they didn't look chagrined. They just looked pissed off. At me.

"Wait. Sorry. I forgot," I said. "You don't *have* feelings."

I looked at Daniel as I said this. I don't know why—maybe because I was more disappointed in him than anyone—and his jaw clenched as he stared back at me. I wanted him to say he was sorry. To say *anything*. But he didn't. Finally I turned and stormed off after Jaimee. I had to get out of there before *I* burst into tears.

• • •

I came back down to the rec room a little while later, having calmed Jaimee down enough that she was no longer blowing her nose, but not enough to coax her out of her room. I could hear hushed voices whispering down below as I descended and I held my breath, preparing myself for whatever confrontation might ensue. Terrell? Daniel? Who was going to get on my case first? Hardly mattered. I knew that I was right and I would argue my point until the cows came home.

If we had any cows.

But when I arrived at the bottom of the stairs, I noticed something was missing. The guys. The pizza and the wings were gone as well. Apparently they had taken their food and fled. Nice to know they still had an appetite. Heathens.

Tara and a bunch of the other girls were folding up the last of the tables while Chandra and Kimberly stacked tins of baked goods. Sage, Lindsey and Karianna were all huddled up in the center of the room, whispering.

"Hey," I said quietly.

"You!" Sage whirled on me, crossing her arms over her chest. "What is *wrong* with you?"

Okay. That was one person I was not expecting to volley with. Not that I wasn't used to it.

"What do you mean?" I asked, completely clueless.

"They left!" she exclaimed. "Why did you have to be such a bitch to them?"

"Excuse me! I think she said exactly what needed to be said!" Chandra protested, stepping up next to me.

"You would," Lindsey said, looking Chandra up and down.

"Oh! What was that? Some kind of brunette commentary?" I asked.

"If the mousy brown rat's nest fits," Lindsey said snootily.

"That doesn't even make any sense," Felice said, a little line appearing between her brows.

"Whatever, the point is, the guys are pissed at us now," Karianna said. Like it was the end of the world.

"So what?" Tara asked shrilly. "I'm pissed at *them*. We should *all* be pissed at them. They came in here, they didn't lift a finger to help us all night, and then they defecated all over Jaimee's hard work. Does that even matter at all to you people?"

"Or are you so dumbstruck with lo-o-ove that you failed to notice one of your teammates running out of here in tears?" Phoebe added.

"How *is* Jaimee?" Autumn asked.

"She's upset," I told her matter-of-factly. "Really upset."

"As she should be," Tara put in.

"Hey! Terrell made a mistake. One mistake," Sage said. "And Annisa treated him and all the other guys like they were serial killers. They're our teammates too."

"Serial killers?" I said. "Hello, hyperbole!"

"Oh, you are so pretentious. Newsflash! Mrs. O'Donaghue isn't here to be impressed with you right now," Sage said. "When are you going to get over yourself already?"

My jaw dropped open. For once, I was rendered totally speechless.

"Okay, you guys?" Autumn interjected. "The vibe in here is getting kind of murky. Why don't we all take a deep breath and—"

"Stick a sock in it, hippie chick," Karianna said with a sneer.

Autumn looked stricken. "There's no need for name-calling."

"Come on, you guys. We can't let *them* divide *us*," I said.

"Listen to the way she says 'them,'" Lindsey said, placing one hand on her ever-jutted-out hip. "Like they're the enemy or something."

"Well, they are if they're going to be responsible for us attacking each other," Tara said. "Especially after how far we've come."

That made everyone pause for a second. This whole year had been about bickering and infighting and having to repair the squad after we tore ourselves to shreds. Once we got through nationals, we had all sort of calmed down and I, for one, had thought all that was over. And maybe it would have been, if Coach Holmes had never brought guys onto the squad.

For once, Tara Timothy and I were on the same side of an argument. Apparently good ol' Hades had finally frozen over.

"Whatever. I'm gonna go call Terrell and make sure he's all right," Sage said.

"Like Terrell Truluck is ever anything but all right," Tara said sarcastically.

Sage grabbed her leather backpack and headed for the stairs. Unbelievable. She wasn't even dating the guy. I was dating Daniel and just then I was still too irritated to care much if he was all right. I mean, he had left without even saying good-bye to me. What was that about?

"And I'm gonna call Joe," Lindsey added.

"Not if I do first," Karianna said, lunging for her purse. They both jockeyed for the stairs, bickering their way up and out as they frantically dialed on their cell phones.

"Well. That was tons of fun," Chandra said once they were gone.

"Witches," Autumn added.

"Autumn!" I said, surprised. So much for no name-calling.

She shrugged. "Well, I feel better now."

Yeah. We were in trouble. Big-time.

All day Sunday I kept waiting for the phone to ring or the doorbell to bong. I figured Daniel owed me an apology. Maybe even more than one. And I was resolved to wait patiently for that apology and to hear him out whenever he decided to grovel. I even imagined my benevolent speech of forgiveness. Which would end with a nice strong closer, like, "Just don't let it happen again."

Not sure I would ever actually say that, but it was fun to imagine.

But the longer Sunday dragged on, the more my forgiving spirit waned. I got through my late breakfast without a peep. Did my homework and nothing. Sat around watching DVDs for four hours and zilch. What was going on here? Daniel called me every single day, unless I called him first. So even if he didn't know I was irritated, he would have called me anyway. Which meant he *did* know I was irritated and was purposely *not* calling me. Was *he* mad at *me* for some reason? That would just be so wrong. I mean, what did *I* do?

Nothing!

Finally, I knew what I had to do. I had a phone call to make. And thankfully, I had free weekends on my cell plan. I turned off the TV, shoved myself up from the couch and held down the speed-dial 1 button. Not even Daniel had bumped my *numero uno* gal down on my dial list.

"Neece!" Jordan Trott, my best friend from New Jersey, screamed in my ear. "I was just thinking about you! Do you have any idea where I am right now?"

"Where?" I asked, trudging toward the kitchen.

"Medieval Times!" she shouted as a huge cheer went up in the background. "It's Maria's birthday!"

"Omigod! The Fourth Annual Cheesefest?" I said, feeling an intense nostalgia for home. Each year Maria Rinaldi celebrated the day of her birth by finding the single cheesiest thing to do and making us all do it with her. We'd participated in video bowling at the Bowl-O-Rama, gone karaoke-ing at PartyWorld, and seen a magician-comedian-ventriloquist at Bananas Comedy Club. But Medieval Times? Maria was really outdoing herself.

"At this very moment I am eating a disgusting turkey leg with my hands while watching two college kids with King Arthur envy pretending to joust each other," Jordan announced. "This rocks!"

I leaned back against the island in the kitchen and stared at my distorted reflection in the stainless steel refrigerator. Somewhere out there my best friend was having the time of her life with a bunch of my other former friends. Meanwhile, I had been, once again, burned by the blondes—a category that, this time, included my tow-haired boyfriend.

"I wish I was there, Jor," I said.

"Me too!" Jordan replied. "Hey. What's the matter?"

"Oh, the usual. Sage called me pretentious in front of everyone."

Jordan snorted. "Oh, I am going to come down there and kick that scrawny little butt of hers all the way to San Juan."

I smiled sadly. "But that's not the worst of it. I think I'm in a fight with Daniel."

"*What?* Hang on a sec."

I heard a lot of jostling, a muffled curse from a guy with a deep voice and then some footsteps. Soon Jordan was back and now there was no background noise on the other end.

"What happened? Talk to Jordan."

So I told her the whole story. About Jaimee and Terrell and the wings and the laughter. My outburst and Daniel's clenched-jaw stare.

"And then he left and didn't even say good-bye," I told her. I took a deep breath and yanked open the refrigerator. Fruit juice, leftover Chinese, a plastic container of hummus. Nothing I wanted. "So, what do you think?"

"We-ell . . . ," Jordan said.

Instantly the hairs on the back of my neck stood on end. I grabbed a slice of Kraft American and held the phone between my ear and shoulder while I unwrapped it. "What?"

"Can I play testosterone advocate?" she asked.

"Please."

"Okay, pretend you're Daniel," she said. "You just spent an entire night negating your manhood to show your girl-friend that you were dedicated to her squad and then she yells at you in front of everyone and says you have no feelings. I mean, this is the guy that just told you he loved you, right? That cuts a little deep."

I felt kind of sick to my stomach and dropped the cheese slice on the counter. "Yeah. But Jor, it's not just *my* squad anymore. It's his too. He doesn't have to prove to me that he's dedicated. He should just *be* dedicated."

"Well, he clearly is. A lot more than those other buttheads," Jordan said.

I snorted a laugh. "Okay, you have a point."

"I'm not saying he was a hundred percent right," Jordan told me. "He shouldn't have laughed. But cut the guy a little slack. He didn't order the wings. He didn't throw the wings. And he didn't *mean* to hurt your friend's feelings. And besides, he *is* completely dreamy. That should count for something in this world."

Slowly, I smiled. "You're sick, you know that?"

"Neece, *everyone* knows that," Jordan joked. "Listen, I should probably get back. They're gonna pick someone to be the princess soon and if I have anything to say about it, it's gonna be me."

"Godspeed, fair maiden," I said.

"Right back at ya."

Out of nowhere, tears prickled behind my eyes. "Jor? I miss you."

"I miss you too," she said quietly. "Bye, Neece."

"Bye."

I hung up the phone, took a deep breath and stared at the sun and moon animation on the screen. Maybe Jordan was right. Maybe *I* should call Daniel. Just one call and I could end this now. But even if I knew that Daniel wasn't a hundred percent wrong and I wasn't a hundred percent right, I still wasn't quite ready to swallow my pride and apologize. I had to think about what I was going to say or it was all going to come out wrong.

So as much as my heart was telling me to hit speed-dial

2, I fought the urge and shoved my phone into my pocket. Tonight it was just me and the cheese. I'd deal with Daniel tomorrow.

● ● ●

Monday morning, I was back in SpaceyVille. (Actor Kevin Spacey, mayor.) After a full night of staring at my bedroom ceiling obsessing, I was not in the mood to deal with primping. So instead I showered, shoved my wet, short brown hair back in a tortoiseshell headband, put on my favorite light blue SDH sweatshirt and headed out for school. It was an unusually chilly morning and I even spotted frost on some of the flowers along the driveway. I was about to turn around and head back for a jacket when I saw Daniel waiting for me by the mailbox. I nearly tripped myself when I saw him standing there. Suddenly I was perfectly warm.

"You okay?" Daniel asked, reaching out as I skipped a few steps forward to catch my balance.

"Fine," I said, striding right by him.

My heart pounded crazily. On one shoulder, my angel screamed at me that I was being immature. *Hello! Last night you decided to apologize, Annisa!* While on the other, the little devil was just snickering.

Heh. Heh. Heh.

I would have reached up to flick the shoulder angel off if it wouldn't have made me look totally insane. How could Daniel just stand there like nothing was wrong? Just seeing him brought the insult of Saturday night back full-force, washing all the rationality away.

"You're mad," he said.

I swung around. "Of course I'm mad! Why didn't you call me yesterday?"

"Uh . . . because I knew you were mad?" Daniel said, shrugging and biting his lip.

Damn. Did he have to be adorable right now? I was trying to be stoic over here.

"Oh, so, what? You just thought if you gave me twenty-four hours, I'd forget all about it?" I asked.

"Didn't work, huh?" he asked.

"Nice try," I told him. Then I turned and started walking again.

"Look, I'm really sorry I laughed, okay?" he said, jogging to catch up with me. "It was more nervous laughter at first, you know? Like I knew you guys were going to explode and I just couldn't help it."

I just kept walking. I knew about nervous laughter. A girl with my Class A klutz status was all *about* nervous laughter. But you didn't laugh at someone else's expense. And you certainly didn't do it in her face when she was crying.

"And you gotta admit," Daniel said. "It *was* kind of funny."

"Ugh!" I blurted, whirling on him. He was grinning. Grinning right at my indignation. Infuriating. "You are such a . . . such a . . . *guy!*"

Daniel blinked, his brow knitting. "Thank you."

Okay. Look. It wasn't that I didn't *want* him to be a guy. Of course I did. I probably wouldn't have been dating him if he *wasn't* a guy. But Daniel had never been *this* sort of guy. This sort of grunty, testosteroney, laugh-at-other-people's-expense guy. What had happened to him? Where was sweet, sensitive Daniel? The one who played the guitar and sang in choir and always bought me one of the warm chocolate chip cookies at lunch. The guy who had skipped school to come down to nationals to show me how much he cared about me. I'll admit it—this whole boyfriend thing was new to me—but were they always so . . . schizo?

"That was not intended to be a compliment," I told him in a huff.

"Annisa, look, the point is, we all feel really bad about the banner. Maybe we didn't react so well at the time, but no one *wanted* to make Jaimee cry."

This echoed what Jordan had said and I paused, feeling slightly guilty for turning the screws.

"Even Terrell feels really bad about it," Daniel said.

I crossed my arms over my chest and held on. It actually helped warm me up a little. "All right then," I said. "What's he going to do about it?"

"What's who going to do about what?" Daniel asked.

I rolled my eyes. "The sign! What's he going to do about it if he feels *so* bad?"

I had never seen Daniel look so blank before. I might as well have just asked him to divide 3477 by the square root of 13.

"What can he do?" he asked finally.

"Well, gee, I don't know," I said sarcastically. "He could help Jaimee make a new banner. Seems pretty obvious to me."

Daniel blew out a scoff. Honestly, if I didn't love him, I might have stomped on his foot. I was being serious here and he was totally blowing me off.

"Come on, Annisa. You know that if the guys walk into the lobby and see some 'Snag the Dolphins' sign that Terrell helped make, he will never hear the end of it," Daniel said, throwing in some facetious air quotes.

"How would anyone *ever* know that Terrell helped make it?" I asked.

"Do you even go to this school? These things kind of have a way of getting out," Daniel replied.

Oh. Now *he* was getting sarcastic with *me*? I don't think so!

"Look. If you guys didn't want to be cheerleaders, then maybe you shouldn't have tried out for the squad," I said.

There. I said it. Take that.

"Geez, Annisa, what's wrong with you?" Daniel said. "You sound like Tara Timothy."

My jaw dropped so fast, it made a gouge in the asphalt at my feet. How dare he compare me to Tara! He *knew* that was hitting below the belt. Was this what we had come to?

"That's it. I'm outta here," I said, turning and striding toward the football field, which we cut across each and every day.

"Annisa—"

"No! You stay at least ten paces behind me, Healy," I said, throwing a hand up behind me as I speed-walked. "Otherwise, I cannot be responsible for my actions."

Nice! My shoulder devil cheered as my nostrils flared.

The angel shook her head and sighed. *This is going nowhere good.*

It wasn't until much later that I realized I had never had a chance to apologize for saying he had no feelings. Once again, Annisa Gobrowski talks before she thinks.

Shocker.

• • •

That afternoon we were supposed to work out in the weight room before a light practice. The guys got there before us and commandeered the good weight benches in the rear corner of the room. Joe was on his back shoving some ridiculous amount of weight up and down above his chest while Terrell spotted him and Daniel and Steven hovered. While Joe worked, the guys muttered amongst themselves. And when we arrived, they turned their backs to us. They couldn't have made it any clearer that they wanted to have nothing to do with us.

"Where do they get off acting like *they* are ignoring *us?*" Tara said under her breath, grabbing a couple of free weights off the rack. She dropped them on the floor, then put her foot up on the barre to stretch, trying to act like nothing was amiss. The rest of the girls gathered around one by one as they trailed through the door. *"They're* the ones who screwed everything up," Tara added.

I couldn't have agreed more. Maybe I *was* turning into Tara Timothy.

Uh, no. Didn't want that. Both because it would be scary *and* because it would prove Daniel right. I hooked my arm behind my head and held on to my elbow, stretching out my triceps.

"Maybe we should have given them a chance to apologize on Saturday," I said, taking a cue from Jordan and playing testosterone advocate. Anything to keep from going over to the dark side.

"We would have if they hadn't cut and run," Chandra reminded me, holding on to the barre as she stretched her quads.

"They were totally immature about the whole thing," Phoebe agreed.

Well. They had me there.

Sage strode into the room with her gym bag and walked right by the rest of us girls. Our heads all whipped around as one, following her progress. She narrowed her eyes at me as she passed by, dropped her bag on the floor near the guys and unzipped her white-and-blue sweatshirt, revealing the pink tank top underneath. She grabbed a pair of ten-pound free weights, dropped down on the weight bench next to Joe's and started in on biceps curls. No one looked more surprised than Terrell when she said hello and started chatting.

Moments later, Lindsey and Karianna broke off and followed Sage's lead, gathering around the guys. Then Michelle and Maureen did the same. Where had *that* come from?

"Real nice," Phoebe said.

"Guess we've officially chosen sides," Chandra added.

Jaimee just looked at her feet, miserable. I wondered how any of the girls who had cheered with her for so long could side with the guys who had sent her into hysterics. Guys who, by the way, had yet to apologize to her.

The door opened and slammed and Coach Holmes paused near the shelf full of stability balls. She wore a hot pink sweatshirt with white-and-yellow trim that was so bright, she could have been spotted from space.

"Hello, everyone," she said, looking from the boys to us and back again. "What's this all about?" She continued to eye our two factions as she walked over to the desk near the wall and placed her portable stereo down on top of it. "You guys were supposed to bond this weekend, not disband."

A thick silence blanketed the weight room, almost as thick as the permanent stench of sweat and feet that always clung to the air. I felt like some giant hand was holding a magnifying glass over us, trying to fry us with a beam of sunlight. Very soon I found myself staring down at my sneakers, as if not looking at Coach Holmes would make her unable to see me.

"Anyone want to tell me what's going on?" Coach said.

I saw Tara's feet move and looked up as she stepped forward. Apparently she had been more than serious when she'd told us she was ready to tattle on the guys. And that had been *before* the banner debacle.

"Here we go," Chandra said.

"We believe that the guys, but especially Terrell, owe Jaimee an apology," Tara stated firmly.

My heart felt like a sheet of paper being crumpled in someone's fist. This was not going to be pretty.

"And why is that?" Coach asked, looking at all of us.

"Because Jaimee spent all night making this amazing banner and then Terrell threw a bag of hot wings at it," Phoebe replied, glaring at the boys.

"Hey! No way!" Terrell cried, walking around the weight bench. "That is *not* how it went down! I threw the wings, yeah, but not *at* the banner. That was a mistake."

"So you admit you ruined Jaimee's hard work," Coach said.

Terrell let out an indignant squeak and shifted his feet. "Well, yeah, but not on purpose."

Coach Holmes nodded and moved away from the wall, standing between our two groups. "I think I understand. Truluck, will you come over here, please?" she said.

Terrell hesitated. My stomach turned.

"Now," Coach said.

Terrell sighed audibly, but strode over to Coach Holmes'

side, his sneakers squeaking on the rubber-padded floor. He stood there, legs apart, arms crossed over his chest, as if daring Coach Holmes to punish him. My skin pulsated to the beat of my heart. I might as well have been witnessing a high-noon standoff. That's how tense I felt.

"Jaimee, you too," Coach Holmes said. No one moved. "Come over here, please."

I glanced at Chandra and she and Felice parted so that Jaimee was visible to the entire room. Her face was as red as a hot coal as she glanced timidly at Terrell and stepped forward. She looked like she was going to burst into tears all over again. For someone who spent a lot of time in the spotlight, she clearly didn't relish this one. Terrell clenched his jaw, but dropped his arms.

"I'm really sorry, Jaimee," he said firmly. "I didn't mean it."

"That's okay," Jaimee said weakly.

I let out a breath of relief. That was easier than I thought it would be. Terrell turned to go back to the comforting company of his cohorts, but Coach Holmes stopped him.

"We're not done here," she said. Terrell tipped his head back, fed up, and turned to her again. "I think you need to help Jaimee make a new banner."

Hey! That's what *I* said!

"Come on, Coach," Terrell said.

"We need a banner. We had a banner. You ruined the banner. I think it's only fair you make a new one," Coach said.

Tara smirked and Chandra laid her hand out for me to slip mine across, which I did. Aw, yeah. That's how we roll.

"No way," Terrell said. "Not gonna happen."

"Excuse me?" Coach asked. The vein in her forehead started to throb.

"If I wanted to spend my time doing artsy-fartsy crap, I would've joined the art club or whatever," Terrell said. "I am an athlete. An *all-state* athlete, in case you didn't hear. I'm here to do stunts and gymnastics and have fun. Not to play Martha Stewart."

"Nice," Joe said.

Holy full-twisting layouts. Did these guys not understand the power of the throbbing vein?

"Where's Coach Rincon, anyway? He'd back me up," Terrell added.

Coach Holmes took a deep breath and massaged her forehead with her thumb and forefinger. "Coach Rincon won't be joining us for practices anymore," she said, earning an audible gasp from the room. I glanced at Chandra. Damn. *Had* we broken them up? "Come on, people, it's not like you're never going to see him again. He *will* be here for the pep rally. Said he wouldn't miss it," she added.

Phew. Okay. At least that was a good sign.

"Great. Now we're down one man," Terrell said. "The odds around here just keep gettin' worse."

Oy. Did this kid enjoy digging himself holes?

"I'm sorry if you don't like your odds, Truluck, but from here on out you deal with me and only me." Coach took a few steps closer to Terrell. He didn't back down an inch. "And I must say, I am sick and tired of your attitude. I asked you all to plan an activity to promote squad unity and clearly you didn't bother to take my request seriously—"

Terrell rolled his eyes. "Coach—"

"Making banners and decorations to rally school spirit is part of being a cheerleader at Sand Dune High, no matter what Coach Rincon had to say on the matter," Coach continued, raising a hand to shut him up. "If you don't like it, you can walk."

Terrell blinked. Clearly he thought he was slightly more indispensable than Coach's comments implied.

"You're not serious," he said.

"Do I look like I'm kidding?" Coach asked.

She didn't. Not even a little bit. And that vein was *definitely* not kidding.

Terrell glanced at the team. We stared back. Everyone in the room held their breath. I wanted to look at Daniel, but that would have involved actual turning of my body and just then I couldn't so much as blink. Plus, there was the fact that we hadn't spoken all day—not since our little meltdown that morning.

Finally, ever so slowly, Terrell smiled. And not in a good way. I had this vision of him as a larger-than-life supervillain in a black cape, snarling down at Coach Holmes.

"Screw this," he said, backing up from Coach and throwing his hands down. "If that's the way you want to play it, then fine. I walk."

He spun on his heel and strode across the room. I turned a wide-eyed look at Chandra and Autumn, who were next to me. Phoebe and Tara slapped hands behind their backs. Unbelievable. Never in my life had I seen someone talk back to an authority figure like that. Especially not one like Coach Holmes. Even the strongest of beings cowered before her.

But honestly, I was almost relieved to see Terrell go. As much as I had always liked the guy, he was a serious thorn in the foot of this cheerleading squad. Among the guys he was the agitator. Maybe that would be his supervillain name. Yeah. The Agitator. He'd have a big A on his chest and he'd be hovering over a huge vat of boiling lava, stirring us all up inside while he laughed his evil supervillain laugh.

Maybe we would all be better off without him.

"You sure about this, Truluck?" Coach Holmes shouted.

His response was to shove through the heavy metal door and slam it as hard as he possibly could.

• • •

"He has a lot of anger," Autumn said a couple of hours later as we went for a water break. "You can see it in his aura. Black splotches everywhere."

"Yeah, well, you'd have to have a lot of anger to be able to stand up to Coach Holmes like that," I said, leaning back against the cool wall next to the water fountain. "And bravery. And maybe a little bit of a death wish."

Daniel, Joe and Steven walked out of the weight room and gathered around the vending machine in silence. Tension instantly filled the gym lobby. They all pointedly ignored us as they fed their quarters into the slot and snagged their drinks. I felt like I was back in kindergarten when boys thought girls were icky and we all stayed on opposite ends of the playground. What was next? A fingerpaint fight?

"What's their problem?" Jaimee asked quietly. "They've been like that all practice."

"They lost their fearless leader," Chandra said grumpily.

I reached out and rubbed Jaimee's bare arm in sympathy. I knew the guys' new freeze-them-out attitude was especially hard on her, since she and Steven had been best friends all their lives. Of course it was kind of tough on me too. Since one of the freezers was supposedly the love of my life.

I tried to catch Daniel's eye, but he was pointedly keeping his attention trained on his soda selection. Once they all had their drinks, they took them outside onto the cold stucco steps. So much for things getting better with Terrell gone. Our whole practice had been off-kilter as Coach Holmes was clearly frustrated, trying to reconfigure our stunts and pyramids for three guys rather than four. Meanwhile, the guys spoke to us only when they absolutely had to and refused to even look at us otherwise. If anything, things had only gotten worse.

"And then there were three," Tara said under her breath. She was being a little *too* gleeful about our sucky situation, if you asked me.

"Typical Tara Timothy," Sage said, shaking her head as she stepped up to the water fountain.

We sucked in a collective breath as Tara's eyes narrowed. If standing up to Coach Holmes was the most dangerous thing a person could do around here, standing up to Tara was second.

"What's that supposed to mean, Barnard?" Tara snapped.

Sage just blithely bent over the water fountain, took a long drink, then stood up and wiped her lips with the tips of her fingers. She slowly pushed her thick French braid over her shoulder. The scathing look she cast around at the rest of us was worthy of a Disney villain. Seriously, those animators needed to give her a call and use her as a model or something.

"It means I hope you guys are proud of yourselves," she

said, facing Tara and Phoebe. "Not only did you get our best guy kicked off the squad, but you've completely annoyed the rest of them. I wouldn't be surprised if they were all out of here by the end of the day. They're probably talking about quitting right now."

"Thank God," Tara said.

Oh, God. Are they? I wondered, glancing through the glass doors. It sucked not knowing what was going on in Daniel's head. It sucked not being able to talk to him. Everything about this sucked.

"Real nice," Sage said to Tara. "Even you have to admit that having them on the team completely elevated the level of this squad."

"No, I don't," Tara said. Her face went from pink with exertion to red with anger in no time flat. "I don't have to admit that. Are you guys forgetting where we were a month ago? We are national champions. National champions! And we did it without *them*. You can't get much more elevated than that!"

And that was when I saw it. The real reason Tara was so irritated about the guys. In her mind she had led our squad to a national title. Coach Holmes bringing the guys onto the squad messed with her ego. It implied that all Tara's hard work wasn't enough. It implied that we could still improve. To Tara, she had already made us the best we could be.

Tara was taking the guys as a personal insult.

Still, no one could argue with her point. We *were* the number-one team in the nation. Without the help of any men. Even Karianna and Lindsey looked a bit moved at the invoking of our recent triumph.

"Whatever. Everyone at the other schools already saw us

out there with the guys at the tournament," Sage said. "West Wind is expecting us to bring them to the rivalry game. When we walk out there and it's just us, we're going to look like a bunch of idiots who talked a big game, but couldn't get it done. Plus, we don't even have a routine for a sixteen-girl squad. We'll have to recycle something from *last season*."

Everyone stared either at the floor or at each other. If Tara knew how to rile us, Sage knew how to hit us where it hurt. She was right. If we went out on West Wind's court for the rivalry game with last season's routine, against the former district cheerleading champs whom we had unseated, everyone was going to think our nationals victory was just a fluke. That we were phoning it in. That we were over.

"The West Wind Dolphins are going to laugh us off the court," Sage said finally, looking at Phoebe. "And you and your big, fat tattletale mouth are going to be the ones to blame."

She might as well have just dropped an A-bomb on the school. I watched as all the blood rushed to Phoebe's face. "Who the hell do you think you are, sophomore?" she snapped, getting all up in Sage's face so that their noses practically touched. "We'll kick you off this squad so fast, it'll blow your highlights out."

"Phoebe! Come on!" Tara said, slack-jawed.

"Get away from me, freak!" Sage cried.

"Make me!" Phoebe shouted.

"Fine!" Sage replied.

And then she shoved Phoebe backward with both hands.

For a split second, no one moved, and then suddenly Chandra, Tara and I were holding Phoebe back, trying to keep her from clawing Sage's eyebrows off. I had never seen her so wigged. Apparently all the pressure had finally gotten to her. Sage had picked the wrong cheerleader to pick on.

"Phoebe! Chill!" Tara shouted.

"Let go of me, Tara," Phoebe replied, struggling. She managed to reach out and grab ahold of Sage's T-shirt, tearing at the collar.

"What's going on out here?"

The commotion had drawn the attention of the wrestling coach, Mr. Gallucci, who was now taking in the scene all baffled. Maybe there was no proper procedure in the school handbook for breaking up a catfight, because he appeared to be rooted to the spot. The door behind him opened and Christopher Healy's head popped through.

"Sage! Phoebe! What're you doing?" he shouted, running out to protect his girlfriend.

"You guys! You gotta see this!" another of the wrestlers shouted with glee.

The doors of the auxiliary gym were thrown open and the wrestling team emptied out, all sweaty and grimy, to watch the girl-against-girl festivities. Before I knew it, Coach Holmes was there blowing her whistle, Daniel was shielding me from someone's flailing arms (my hero) and K.C. had grabbed Phoebe's hands and was holding them behind her back. Christopher, meanwhile, had Sage pinned against the wall, trying to calm her down.

"You okay?" Daniel asked me, all concern.

"Yeah," I said with a small, apologetic, grateful smile. As of that second, I was no longer mad at him. As of that second, I just wanted to do whatever I could to make sure everything went back to normal. 'Cause let's face it, things had definitely gotten out of control. "Thanks for coming to the rescue."

He grinned back. "Anytime."

Apparently Daniel was on the same page as me—right smack in the middle of the forgiveness chapter of *Relationships for Beginners.*

Behind us, Coach Holmes and Coach Gallucci attempted to sort it all out. Coach sent the entire squad to the locker room, minus Sage, Phoebe and Tara, whom she decided to keep behind for questioning.

"What the heck happened?" Daniel asked me, slipping his arm over my shoulders as we headed for the gym.

I sighed as Coach Holmes made Sage and Phoebe shake hands and make up. Though neither looked very happy doing it.

"Nothing good," I replied.

All right, people! Let's talk!" Tara shouted, calling the locker room to attention. Instantly everyone stopped whispering and speculating over what we had just witnessed and turned their attention to the live show. Sage and Phoebe huffed into the room ahead of Tara and dropped down on opposite benches, turning their knees away from each other. Sage crossed her arms over her chest and slumped like a little kid in time-out. Phoebe snapped the hair band she had wrapped around her wrist over and over again.

A gray cloud rolled in over the locker room, bringing with it a rather suffocating humidity. Our energy had officially been sapped by the drama. Tara, however, had a serious manic power coming off of her in bursts. Her eyes were unusually wide as she took us all in, like a spooked horse about to bolt.

Not a good look for her. And it didn't bode well for any of us either.

"Okay, listen up," Tara said, pacing back and forth in front of us. I watched her thigh muscles flex under her short-shorts to keep from making eye contact with her and drawing her ire. "This ends here. I will not have a redux of football season. This is my senior year. This is my *last* season. And I am not going out like this, you got me? There will be no infighting on this squad. From here on out, we are going to have fun, we are going to work hard, and we are going to conduct ourselves like mature adults."

At this, everyone looked at Sage. She turned ten shades of purple, but didn't look up.

"So, I've decided that this coming Saturday, I am going to host the first slumber party of the season so that we can all chill out together and have a little fun," Tara said, still pacing. A quick murmur of delight swept through the room. Nothing piqued a girl's interest like a good slumber party. And I, for one, was shocked that our no-nonsense leader was focusing any of her energy on fun-having. "We'll watch a movie, we'll make some cookies, we'll stay up all night. It'll be great. Just like old times."

Actually she sounded more like a politician going over a platform than a girl psyched for a party, but I'd take whatever I could get.

"Like old pre-guy times," Chandra put in, very much on board. In fact, most of the squad was jumping right on Tara's positivity train.

Karianna pushed herself away from the locker she'd been leaning her shoulder on. "Wait a minute. What *about* the guys?"

Tara paused. "I don't want to hear about them. This is about us. And therefore, they will not be invited."

"Obviously," Phoebe said, snapping that hair band. I wished she would stop already. She had a red welt growing on her skin.

"This weekend is going to be strictly girls-only," Tara reiterated.

Challenge me and die, her tone implied.

Had she forgotten that Coach Holmes had made it clear that she wanted us to be one cohesive team? Having an anti-testosterone fiesta wouldn't go very far to promote that. In fact, it would pretty much obliterate it entirely.

"Uh . . . Tara?" Autumn said tentatively. "Do you really think this is the best idea?"

"Yeah. Coach is kind of all about the 'one team' thing," I put in. "Leaving them out could be bad."

"How about this?" Tara said. Her nostrils flared. "How about you guys let me deal with one crisis at a time? There are far more of us and *clearly* we are falling apart. I'd like to get this part of the team fixed. Then maybe I'll worry about *them.*"

A few people murmured their agreement, but Autumn looked as skeptical as I felt. I had a feeling Tara would never deal with *them* at all, if she could avoid it. But then, I couldn't argue with her one-problem-at-a-time logic. It seemed like a practical approach to a complicated issue. And besides, everyone was already chatting about the party, making plans. The gray storm cloud had officially lifted. This party could prove to be just what the doctor ordered.

I just hoped the guys would understand.

• • •

"What's the Spanish word for 'uneven'?" Bethany whispered to me the next day in the library. She paged through her dog-eared and super-graffitied Spanish dictionary, flattening the spine on the table with a crack. "Any clues? Thoughts? Random guesses?"

Señorita Marquez, our young, desperate-to-prove-she-was-hip Spanish teacher, had allowed us to spend the class period in the library working on her latest sadistic assignment, translating popular songs from English into Spanish. I had a feeling she thought we'd all *love* the task—that we'd think it was cool and different and all—but really it was torture. We even had to find ways to make them rhyme and everything. Personally, I'd much rather be back in the classroom, asking Bethany, *"Invita usted a sus amigos a su casa?"* for the ten-millionth time.

Okay, so I was feeling a bit negative this morning. After yesterday's practice and second period's failed chemistry experiment (I was lucky I still had sensation in my fingertips, that's all I'm saying), I just wanted *one* thing to be stress-free. And this was *not* it. But at least I was getting to spend an entire class period sitting next to Daniel, playing footsies under the table.

A silver lining to every cloud.

"What song are you doing?" Daniel asked her.

" 'People Are Strange,' " Bethany replied, gnawing on a mushy candy-less lollipop stick.

"Your personal anthem?" he asked.

Suddenly the toe of her boot slammed into my shin.

"Ow! Bethany!" I cried, yanking my leg away from Daniel's.

"Shhhh!" Señorita Marquez and the elderly librarian behind the counter hissed in unison.

"Sorry!" I whispered at them. I reached down and rubbed at my shin. "Ugh. That's gonna leave a mark."

"Sorry," Bethany said, pressing her lips together. "I thought I was kicking *him.*" She gestured at Daniel with her lollipop stick and a wad of pulpy, mashed stick plopped onto the table.

"Ew," I said.

"Might as well have." Daniel took my hand and squeezed my fingers. "You kick my girl, you kick me."

Awww. Pain erased. I loved it when he called me "his girl." Bethany noticed my goofy grin and made a gagging sound.

"I need to be constantly mainlining Alka-Seltzer around you two," she said, slamming her book closed. "I'm gonna go ask Marquez. Don't be swapping saliva when I get back," she said, pointing her black-gloved finger from me to Daniel and back again.

I sat back in my chair and sighed as Bethany loped away. "Where did she get this psycho idea to have us translate songs?" I asked, staring at the blank page in front of me. All I had so far was the title of mine, "Señorita Independiente," a Kelly Clarkson classic. I was having a hard time concentrating, considering the ten billion other things on my mind. Like the fact that I had to tell Daniel about this weekend's slumber party before he found out through the grapevine. The last thing we needed right now was another "why didn't you tell me?" conversation. I wasn't sure either one of us could take it.

"I think it's kinda cool," Daniel said, lifting a shoulder. "Better than another in-class conversation about where the bathroom is and how to find the post office."

I smirked. Sometimes, in the middle of the school day, I just wanted to reach out and run my fingers through Daniel's hair. But I restrained myself. Most of the time.

"So, are you going to K.C.'s match on Saturday?" Daniel asked, reaching out and toying with my heart bracelet. "I was thinking maybe we could hang out."

Gulp. Saturday. I guess it was about time to tell him what was going on.

"Actually, I don't think I can," I said, sliding my butt back on the smooth wooden chair to sit up straight. "Listen, Daniel, there's something I have to tell you."

"Oh. This doesn't sound good," he said, swallowing hard.

"Oh! No! It's not big deal," I whispered. "It's just . . . Tara's having a slumber party for the squad this weekend."

For a split second his eyes lit up. I had a feeling that visions of half-dressed girls and pillow fights danced through his head.

"Girls only," I added firmly.

And the eyes went dead.

"What? Seriously?" he said.

"Yeah. I know," I told him. "It's just after the fight yesterday, she kind of thought it would be a good idea for the team to bond."

"Uh, right. And me and Joe and Steven are on the team too," he said. "At least we were the last time I checked."

"Well, it's just something we always do," I told him, trying to put a positive spin on it. "Slumber parties are like a tradition. But we can't exactly have guys there . . ."

"Right, so maybe we should start a new tradition," Daniel said tersely. "Something the whole squad could do together. Did she ever think of that?"

I bit my bottom lip and slumped again. The guy had a point. Of course he did. I had thought the same thing myself. But Tara had made up her mind. And we all knew that when

Tara made up her mind, you couldn't change it without a lobotomy.

"She just wants us to do something fun together. You know, to kind of erase the whole fight thing," I said. "And to be honest, part of me agrees with her. I mean, it's bad enough that the guys and girls can't seem to get along, but now the girls aren't getting along with the girls. If this keeps up, the whole squad is going to self-destruct."

Daniel took a deep breath. His eyes were like swirls of blue-green seawater. "This really means a lot to you, huh?"

"Yeah. It kind of does," I said, touched that he understood.

"It just sucks," he said, though with slightly less venom now. "Like we didn't feel enough like lepers already."

"Well, it's just one night," I told him. "And then maybe next week we can figure out something we can all do together."

Daniel forced a smile. "Yeah. Maybe."

Just then Bethany stumbled back toward the table, one hand over her eyes, walking into chairs and bookshelves as she went. History books teetered from their displays and fell; a stand full of pamphlets on the importance of reading slammed into the floor and fanned out over the carpet. Señorita Marquez rolled her eyes closed and sank down in her seat as the librarian went ashen.

"I'm back. You can stop making out now!" Bethany announced.

"Shhhhh!" the entire class scolded her as she slammed hip-first into a book cart.

"Miss Goow. Do I have to give you a detention?" the librarian asked.

"You don't *have* to do anything in this life, Ms. Gruber," Bethany replied. "That's why they call this America."

Daniel and I laughed and just like that, the tension was broken. I'd have to thank Bethany later. And maybe add a swift kick to the shin.

• • •

That afternoon half the school huddled inside the lobby, staring out the normally sun-drenched glass doors and windows at the monsoon that raged outside. The buses had already lined up at the curb, their headlights on and their windshield wipers thwap, thwap, thwapping away. One brave soul lifted his denim jacket above his head and shouted as he dove into the rain and ran for his car. We all watched with interest. By the time he got there, he looked like he'd just gotten off a waterslide.

"I thought the weather guy said it was going to be in the mid-seventies and sunny," Autumn said, shivering as another intrepid senior opened the door and let in a burst of cold air. We were both dressed for practice in the cafeteria and goose bumps had already broken out on all my exposed parts.

"He did," Bethany said, fishing in her bag and pulling out a half-mangled umbrella. "The loser."

"It's like something out of a disaster movie," I said. *"The Storm That Ate Sand Dune."*

"I think I'm gonna be a weather person," Bethany said. "I just decided."

"Why?" Autumn and I asked in unison.

"It's, like, the only job where you can be totally wrong every single day and still keep your job," she said. "I like that kinda gig."

I could just see Bethany up there in front of the weather board with her thick black eyeliner and rainbow-color-of-the-day hair. She'd probably make shadow puppets and have her fingers devour the Midwest or something.

"Wish me luck," she said, heading for the doors.

"Luck!" we both shouted.

The door to the cafeteria opened and Chandra waved manically at us. "You guys! Come on! She already started stretching!"

Autumn and I looked at each other and sighed. We both knew that the only reason we were still standing out here among the masses was that we were dreading practice. By now all the guys had heard about the slumber party and we just *knew* it was going to create new and different forms of tension.

"Guess we can't avoid it forever," I said.

"If only we could find a rift in the space-time contin-uum," Autumn said.

I nodded. "If only."

Together we trudged our way through the crowd and into the relative emptiness of the caf, taking our spots in line.

"You're late!" Coach called out.

"Sorry, Coach!" we both replied.

As Tara led us in stretching, the rain pelted the cafeteria windows. I could barely hear her counts over all the weather-related noise and we kept flinching every time there was a loud gust of wind or a clap of thunder. We were all doing hamstring stretches, standing on one foot like a flock of skittish storks, when the door to the cafeteria squealed its way open. Sage actually fell sideways and almost took Karianna out in the process when Terrell walked in, a scroll of white paper tucked under his arm. Everyone dropped their feet and Tara turned around to see what had made us all blanch. A flash of lightning blinded the otherwise dim room, followed by a low rumble of thunder.

"Truluck! What are you doing here?" Coach asked.

"I thought you quit," Tara put in.

Bring on the drama.

"What's going on?" I hissed at Daniel.

But I knew from the stunned look on his face that even he hadn't expected this visit. He lifted his shoulders and we all took a discreet step forward, trying to hear over the storm.

"I came to apologize, Coach," Terrell said, his voice firm and clear as a bell. He must have spoken very loudly for his words to reach all of us. Always mindful of his audience, that Terrell. He cleared his throat. "I'm hoping you'll let me back on the squad."

Coach was seriously nonplussed. For once she looked like she had no idea what to say. No matter, though. Seemed like Terrell was more than ready to take center stage and hold on to it with all his might.

"I made this," he told her.

He took out the scroll and unfurled it on the floor at Coach Holmes' feet. Instantly everyone broke formation and gathered around Coach Holmes, no longer trying to hide our curiosity.

"Whoa," Chandra said softly.

Jaimee snorted a laugh, then slapped her hand over her mouth when she drew a bunch of scathing stares. I understood where she was coming from, though. It was kind of hard not to laugh. Terrell had made a brand-new banner for the lobby. At least he had *tried* to. He had copied Jaimee's original design, but his artwork was seriously hurting. Like my three-year-old second cousin Tristan could have done a better job. But his lettering was pretty solid and it was clear he'd put a lot of effort into it. Plus, he'd probably had to shop for the paper and the paint after leaving practice yesterday, and as far as I knew, most guys didn't even have a clue where to buy that stuff, so it probably took some time. Once everyone got past the Picasso-esque dolphin and crab, I think we all understood the amount of pride Terrell had forced himself to swallow to do this. He'd even signed his work in the corner, announcing to the world that he was ready and willing to take whatever ribbing the guys of the school chose to throw at him.

Maybe there was hope for Terrell yet.

"I really am sorry, Coach," Terrell said.

"Oh, please," Tara whispered derisively.

"As a peace offering, it's not bad," Coach said with a thoughtful frown. "Okay, Truluck. Go get warmed up."

"What?" Tara blurted, her voice pitched so high, it was earsplitting.

"Don't start with me, Timothy," Coach said, holding up a hand. "Not today."

Terrell clapped his hands and grinned as Joe slapped his back. Uh-oh. Already the mischievous glint had returned to Terrell's eyes, and the rest of the guys responded with gleeful smiles. How did Coach not see it? All the girls on the squad did. I could *feel* the trepidation permeate the room. Maybe Terrell had made the effort and the self-sacrifice, but now that he was back, who knew what trouble he would cause?

Lightning illuminated the room, accompanied by a tremendous clap of thunder, and we all jumped. Evil portent, anyone?

"But Coach—" Tara protested.

"I told Terrell what he'd have to do to make it up to the team and he did it. Therefore, he deserves a second chance," Coach told Tara, cutting her off. "I'd do the same for anyone else on this team."

Tara clenched her jaw, but said nothing.

"Now I believe you were in the middle of stretching?" Coach said.

"Yes, Coach," Tara said.

"Good," Coach replied with a nod. "Get back to it."

As we all shuffled into formation, the guys welcomed Terrell back onto the squad with hand clasps and shoulder bumps. Daniel looked really happy, so I was happy for him. But at the same time, I couldn't help feeling that the guys were a little *too* happy. As if they were looking forward to getting in line behind Terrell again. The villain in his billowing cape.

I just hoped I was wrong.

"What *is* this song?" I shouted to be heard over the blaring stereo at Tara Timothy's house that weekend. I had just returned from a bathroom run to find most of the squad dancing on the furniture like possessed people. Tara, Phoebe, Felice and Kimberly were all bouncing on the ancient couch in Tara's family room, their faces green from Autumn's homemade avocado masks. Over the speakers some weird guy was shouting about june bugs and razorbacks to the tune of seriously funky music.

"It's the B-52's!" Phoebe shouted, doing an awkward version of the twist as the couch cushions shifted beneath her feet. "Come on! Dance!"

Chandra walked by with a bowl full of raw cookie dough, her head bopping up and down to the beat while she ate with a huge wooden spoon. Autumn sat on a cushy chair, braiding Sage's hair in a zillion tiny braids as Sage kept the beat with her feet. Everyone else was getting down like we were in the middle of *American Idol* fifties night, doing the swim and flailing around.

"Um, we never did this last season. Were you guys just saving the really freaky stuff until after you completely sucked me in?" I asked as I allowed Phoebe to pull me up onto the couch. She started bumping my butt until I almost fell right back down.

"This is not freaky!" Phoebe protested. "It's necessary!"

"How, exactly?" I asked as her bony hip smacked into my butt.

"The B-52's are a therapeutic band," Kimberly explained. "You can't *not* be happy when you listen to them."

"And if there's one thing this squad needs, it's guaranteed happy," Felice put in, handing me a virgin piña colada with a crazy straw sticking out of it.

"Well, it appears to be working," I shouted.

"Aw, yeah!" Chandra replied, earning a round of cheers.

I laughed and danced as I sucked down my drink. Time to get fully in the spirit of the moment. And the spirit was high, high, high. Tara's slumber party was definitely doing the trick. We had been here for three hours already and there had been zero fights and zero snarky comments—that I knew about, anyway. Just a lot of junk food eating and stupid game playing and gossip sharing. And now that it was getting late and everyone was punchy and second-winded, the wacky dancing had broken out.

"Know who else is therapeutic? Liz Phair!" Chandra shouted.

"Yeah, but only for breakups," Shira replied, dropping down onto her seriously faded Garfield sleeping bag as the song came to an end.

"No way! She's good for anything!" Chandra protested, offering Lindsey the wooden spoon. "At least her old stuff is."

"I'm a Fiona girl myself," Wendy said.

"Please! Avril all the way!" Ally put in.

About a half dozen pillows and groans were launched in her direction and Ally laughed. "I was *kidding!*"

"What's wrong with Avril?" Jaimee asked.

And thus, the girl-rocker debate began. I dropped down from the couch and grabbed a spoon to partake of the cookie dough while everyone else debated whether Madonna counted as either a girl *or* a rocker. It was all very enlightening, actually.

"All right! You're done," Autumn told Sage as she finished off the last braid.

"You look like Medusa," Karianna told Sage, sticking her tongue through her teeth.

"Maybe. But when she takes it out, she'll be all Jessica Simpson," Jaimee put in. Sage gave a triumphant smile from behind her face mask and grabbed a handful of Doritos from a plastic bowl on the table.

"Jessica Simpson. Now *there's* a rocker," Ally joked, earning another rain of pillows.

"Who wants blue toenails?" Autumn announced, whipping out a bottle of glittery blue nail polish.

"I do!" about ten of us shouted, thrusting our hands into the air.

"One at a time," Autumn said. "I'll do Annisa first."

I plopped down in front of her and offered up my bare toes. Autumn shook the polish up with a grin as the music switched over to some classic rock tune. Apparently Tara was in charge of the music in her own house and she had some seriously eclectic tastes.

"This is working," Autumn said to me quietly. "Don't you think it's working?"

I looked around the room at all the giggling, happy, chatty

faces. "Definitely," I replied. "Look. Even Phoebe and Sage aren't trying to kill each other."

Over on the couch, Phoebe was inspecting Sage's braids with a studious frown. Meanwhile, Sage stuffed enough Doritos into her mouth to feed a small island nation. Her fingers and lips were caked with cheese dust, making her look fairly freak-clownish with the green face and the hair. I had to hand it to her. She really didn't care what she looked like—when there were no guys around.

"Nothing like a girls'-night-in to cure all woes," Autumn said with a smile.

"You can say that again," I replied.

Suddenly there was a slam, then a shriek, then the music died. I glanced at Autumn, wide-eyed. Were we under siege or something?

"Hey! Did someone say there was a slumber party going on tonight!?"

Oh no. No no no no no.

"Daniel?"

I turned around and sure enough, Daniel, Terrell, Joe, Steven and K.C. were all standing in the doorway to the family room in matching SDH sweats, toting sleeping bags and pillows. Apparently, we *were* under siege.

"Party-crashing time! Ready? Okay!" Terrell announced, thrusting his hands on his hips and cracking himself up. He whipped out his cell phone and started snapping pictures, starting with Sage's scary self. "Oh, man. The guys are gonna *love* these!" he said as the flash popped.

"Nooooo!" Sage wailed, diving for her sleeping bag.

"Omigod! Omigod, omigod, omigod," Jaimee cried.

Suddenly girls were running everywhere, grabbing throw

172

pillows to hide their green faces from Terrell's camera. A few closest to the door raced for the bathroom. Felice threw a sweatshirt on over her skimpy nightgown and Kimberly wrapped herself in a blanket to hide her tank and short-shorts.

"What're you guys doing here?" I asked, standing up.

"Crashing the party!" Steven said matter-of-factly. "Was that not clear?"

Daniel took one look at me and cracked up laughing. "Nice look you got there, babe," he said.

Terrell laughed and snapped my picture. My hands flew to the green crust on my face. Suddenly I recalled that my short hair had been pulled back from my forehead in a pink Hello Kitty rubber band and was sticking straight up like a fountain. I looked down at my red flannel nightshirt and half-painted nails and pretty much wanted to die. I half expected my overheated skin to start melting the face mask off in grody clumps.

"Where are you sending those?" I asked Terrell, mortified.

"Oh, just to the entire football, wrestling, basketball and track teams," Terrell said, then looked at Daniel. "Did I leave anyone out?"

"Not that I can think of, no," Daniel replied with mock seriousness.

This was just perfect. First my nearly bare butt appears on the front page of the school newspaper during my first month here, now every guy in Sand Dune was going to have a shot of my freaky green face. Of course the only guy I *really* cared about seeing me look disgusting was standing right in front of me. How badly did this suck?

"You! All of you! Out!" Tara said, storming over to the guys.

But Terrell and Joe had already infiltrated the room. Terrell was busy trying to drag a shrieking Sage out of her sleeping bag by her waist while Joe was flirting with Kari-anna, one of the few face-mask-less people, over by the door to Mr. Timothy's home office. Daniel and K.C. walked around the couch and sat down next to Kimberly, who drew her legs in and curled into the corner under her blanket like she was afraid they might give her cooties. Daniel grabbed a handful of chips and munched on them happily. K.C. put his feet up and spread his arms out across the back of the couch.

Did the mayhem all around them not filter through to their guy brains?

"This is my house and you were *not* invited," Tara told Daniel.

"Come on, Tara. This is a *squad* slumber party," Daniel said with a smirk, popping a chip into his mouth. "I'm on the squad, too."

"Right. And who died and made K.C. a cheerleader?" I said. "No offense," I added to K.C.

"None taken," he replied with a casual smile.

"Well, we just came from his wrestling match, where he recorded his eighth win of the season," Daniel said. "Still undefeated."

"Yeah, baby!" Terrell shouted as Daniel and K.C. slapped hands.

"So we thought he deserved a party," Daniel said. "Especially since only four cheerleaders showed up to support him. And who were those four cheerleaders?" he asked.

"We were!" Terrell, Steven and Joe chorused from around the room.

"Exactly," Daniel said. "Now, where can I get one of those super-cool face masks you're all wearing?"

Steven laughed and Terrell gave up on Sage long enough to slap Daniel's hand. Daniel just grinned all cockily, caught up in the triumph of the moment. Like he was *so* cool. God, testosterone was noxious sometimes. I mean, how could Daniel do this? He knew how important this was to the girls on the squad. To me. How could he ruin it like this?

"Hey! What're you doing? Karianna!" Lindsey shouted.

We all turned around just in time to see Joe and Karianna slipping into Mr. Timothy's office and closing the door behind them. Lindsey gave chase, but she got there just a second too late and the door slammed in her face. We heard a giggle and a click and Lindsey's face crumbled.

"Oh no you're not!" she shouted. She pounded on the door with the heel of her hand. "Karianna! Get out here! Get out here right now!"

"This is not happening," Tara said, her shoulders slumping. Upstairs we could hear several girls all jockeying for the bathroom so they could wash off their faces. Shira struggled to shove her embarrassingly juvenile sleeping bag under the couch and a few other girls huddled in the kitchen, throwing on more clothes.

"Karianna! If you don't come out of there right now, that's it! We are no longer friends!" Lindsey announced, near tears.

Wow. She must have really liked Joe. Why, I had no idea. The guy never spoke except to tell us the things that he didn't do. If there was a senior class award for Biggest Lack of Personality, he would win it in a landslide.

"Okay. Fine!" Lindsey shouted. She turned around, gathered her things up in her arms and stormed out, face mask and all. Her pink sleeping bag trailed behind her and she tripped over it on her way to the front door, losing one of her fuzzy slippers in the process.

"Lindsey! Don't!" Tara called after her.

Lindsey picked up the slipper and two seconds later the door slammed. Hard.

"What is *wrong* with you guys?" I demanded. "Do you have to ruin *everything*?"

"Ruin? Actually, I think we just busted up a seriously lame party," Terrell said, stepping over to stand next to the couch and his cohorts. He crossed his arms over his chest all manly-like. As if there was no way I could contradict him.

"Maybe it's lame to you guys, but it's not lame to us! We were having fun! And now Lindsey's gone and you made her cry and you're sending awful pictures of everyone all over the place and half the squad is upstairs freaking out," I said. "Why couldn't you just leave us alone for *one* night?"

"Dude. I had no idea your girlfriend was such a buzzkill," Terrell said to Daniel.

I wanted to smack him, Susan Lucci style. I waited for Daniel to defend me, but much to my horror, he smirked.

He actually smirked.

"What's the big deal, Jersey? We're just having a little fun," he said, lifting his shoulders. "Remember fun? You used to know how to have it."

The guys all snickered. Daniel might as well have punched me in the stomach. With a wrecking ball. He was mocking me in front of everyone. When I was already upset. He didn't understand anything. He didn't even realize he'd done anything wrong. Even though half the squad was either hiding or had already bailed, he thought this whole thing was totally funny. And he thought it was just fine to pick on me in the middle of it all.

"I have to go," I said, turning around to grab my overnight bag.

"Annisa, I was just kidding," Daniel said cajolingly. "Stay."

Like it could be taken back that easily. He reached for my hand, but I pulled away. I turned and looked him dead in the eye. "I don't really see any good reason to."

His face fell and Terrell let out a surprised "Oh!" Like *"Burn!"* Daniel looked at me like I had completely betrayed him.

Yeah, I thought. *See how it feels.*

Then I got out of there before the shoulder angel and devil could chime in. I had a feeling that, very soon, they would both have a lot to say.

• • •

The rest of the weekend was agony. I kept waiting for Daniel to call and break up with me, so every time the phone rang, I nearly peed in my pants. Plus, there were moments— moments when I replayed his little "Remember fun?" line in my head—that *I* wanted to break up with *him.* I mean, who talks to his girlfriend like that? Where did this sudden mean streak come from?

But then I'd remember all the amazing things he did for me when I first moved to Sand Dune, our first date, our first kiss, that incredible Christmas gift, the I-love-yous, and I'd cave all over again. I spent almost all day Sunday alone in my room, listening to music, taking the bracelet he'd given me on and off and going schizo.

I love him, I hate him, I love him, I hate him, I love him, I hate him.

It was all so exhausting that I fell asleep at eight o'clock. I didn't even get to see what happened in the Sunday night NFL playoff game. I had to watch the crappy highlights on SportsCenter that morning. Just not the same.

I had no idea what to hope for when I walked out of my house on an unbearably sunny Monday morning, but as angry as I still was, I was disappointed when he wasn't waiting for me. I trudged my way to school and when I saw Daniel in the hallway, my heart pretty much stopped beating. Then it died when he took one look at me and walked the other way.

Well. Apparently we knew where *he* stood.

Every second of the day I kept waiting for him to tap me on the shoulder and tell me in no uncertain terms that it was over. What would I do? Would I tell him that was fine by me? Would I break down in tears? Would I flip out on him? Any option was possible at any given moment.

My teachers could have been speaking in Greek. Backward. With pig latin overtones. And I wouldn't have even noticed. It was a total waste of a day.

And then came practice.

We sat on the bleachers in complete silence. I could feel Daniel's eyes burning holes in the back of my T-shirt.

Just break up with me already! I wanted to scream. *Get it over with!*

But I didn't. And he didn't. We just sat there. I glanced at Chandra and she rolled her eyes and blew out a big sigh. Yeah, we all felt it. This was going to be an interesting afternoon.

The moment Coach Holmes stepped into the gym, she

paused. Probably could smell the acrid scent of hatred in the air. Then she strode over to us, all determination, and set the props box down, as always, on the floor in front of us. Like anyone was going to be writing down anything positive today.

"What happened now?" she asked, hands on hips.

I heard a collective intake of breath, but then Holmes lifted a hand, thinking the better of her question.

"On second thought, I don't want to know," she said, waving us off. "Normally I'd never suggest this so early in the game, but this has already been the longest season of my life, so I'm gonna do it. Let's open the props box."

I squirmed in my seat and a bunch of the other girls did the same. I wasn't sure if this was a good idea or a bad one. I had only put a couple of comments in the box over the past few weeks. There couldn't possibly be enough happy thoughts in there to cure the ills of this squad. I wasn't even sure the props box could do that if it was *overflowing* with cheer.

"Come on! It might do you some good to hear the positive things you have to say about each other," Coach said hopefully. "Tara? Want to do the honors?"

With a huff and a dubious sigh, Tara pushed herself up from her seat. She lifted the props box and placed it on the bottom bleacher. Slowly, she detached the tape from around the lid and started to open the box.

"Uh, Coach?" Daniel said, causing my pulse to go berserk.

"Yes, Healy?" she said, raising her eyebrows. "Is there a problem?"

Every cell in my body sizzled. What was he going to say?

Daniel cleared his throat. "Um . . . no," he said finally, though he sounded miserable. "Nothing."

My brow knit together and I automatically turned around to look at him. Even if he did hate me. Even if I maybe did hate him. I had to know. What was that all about?

Daniel looked back at me, his eyes sad. I had never seen his eyes so sad. Then he rolled them up, shook his head and leaned back. He was telling me there was nothing he could do. But about what? *What?*

My heart pounding uneasily, I returned my attention to Tara. I could tell that the props box wasn't nearly as full as it had been the last time we'd opened it—the time that half the comments had suggested I dye my hair blonde for uniformity and my head had spontaneously combusted. All I could do was hope that there was a lot more positivity in there this time around.

Tara lifted out a piece of purple paper. She opened it slowly and read, "'I'm totally psyched to stunt with the guys! We're going to be unstoppable.'" Her voice couldn't have been more flat if it were a popped tire.

Coach Holmes nodded proudly. No one else moved. Whoever had written that had written it before they knew what this season would really be like.

Tara plucked out another piece of paper. "'Props to the guys for their bravery! You deserve to be Mighty Fighting Crabs!'"

Yeah. That one was mine. I had written it after Daniel's confrontation with his brother in the hallway. Figured it would make us both feel better.

Behind me, Daniel sighed. I thought I heard Joe swear.

What was wrong with them? They were getting all the props and acting like it was their funeral.

Tara picked up another piece of paper. When she unfolded it, her face went white so fast, I actually thought she was going to crumple like a tissue.

"Tara?" Phoebe said.

Apparently, I wasn't the only one who noticed.

"'Of all the super sexy squad members, I think I'm the super sexiest,'" she read.

"What?" Coach said.

Tara held up the paper and Coach snatched it out of her hand. As she scanned the page, her forehead vein started to throb. Tara grabbed another piece of paper from the box.

"'Rah, rah, rah. This is dumb as rocks,'" Tara read. "'Rah, rah, rah. The props box sucks.'"

"All right, who did this?" Coach said, nearly shaking. "Who did this?!" The tendons in her neck sprouted and I cringed. Meanwhile, Phoebe, Felice and Sage got up and dove into the box.

"'I think we should all try real, *real* hard to get our GPAs up to one point five this year'?" Felice read. "Nice stereotype, morons. I'm up for valedictorian, in case you hadn't heard."

"Yeah! And Jaimee's, like, the number-one math geek in the state!" Phoebe interjected.

"Thanks. I think," Jaimee said.

"'Let's all get pom-poms permanently tattooed on our butts!'?" Sage read.

"'Props to Tara Timothy! Miss Anal Retentive U.S.A.,'" Tara read.

Someone behind me snorted a laugh. Suddenly everyone was yelling and snatching paper out of the props box. This was way bad. No one messed with the props box. Even I knew that and I wasn't the box's biggest fan.

"What did you do?" I asked through my teeth, whirling around on the guys, who at least had the decency to appear chagrined. Everyone except Terrell, who was trying to hide a smile. "Oh, wait. Don't tell me. You were just having *fun*," I said pointedly.

Suddenly the shrill blare of Coach Holmes' whistle split the room, echoing off the high rafters and freshly waxed floor and slicing through my eardrums. Everyone fell silent and looked at Coach. Littering the floor were dozens of tiny scraps of paper.

"Enough!" Coach shouted, whipping the box away from the crowd. She tossed it on the ground, where it fell on its side, spilling the remainder of its contents out on the basketball court's sideline. "I have never been so disgusted," she said, seething. "You!" she shouted, pointing up at the guys. "Don't even think about trying to claim innocence for this one. I know that these girls did not disrespect our tradition in this way."

I sank lower in my seat, away from the death glare of Coach Holmes. All around me the other girls looked stunned and miserable and angry. Even Sage, Lindsey and Karianna were all clenched.

"I told you guys how important this props box was to the team and what did you do? You ruined it for everyone," Coach continued. "What do you have to say for yourselves?"

No one spoke. No one even moved a muscle. I wouldn't have been surprised if everyone had ceased to swallow, breathe and blink.

"Great. Very mature and manly of you to own up to what

you've done," Coach said sarcastically. "You know what? Practice is canceled. I can't even be around you people right now. Everyone go home."

I glanced uncertainly at Tara. She gaped at Coach Holmes. Coach had never canceled a practice before. Not for as long as I'd known her and apparently not for as long as Tara had known her either. Which was a long time.

"And you four? You think about whether or not you actually want to be a part of this team," Coach continued, pointing a trembling finger at the guys. Trembling with anger. Severe, scary, explosive anger. "I'll expect each of you to answer that question personally to me tomorrow. And if you think I'm kidding, just test me and see what happens."

She grabbed up the fallen box, turned it upside down until it was completely empty and stalked out of the gym. As the door slammed behind her, a huge chasm opened in the gym floor and swallowed us all whole.

Well, not really. But we might have been better off if it had.

I was sitting at my desk in my aqua blue bedroom, my geometry book open in front of me, staring out the window at the leftover Christmas lights on the house across the street, when the phone rang. My heart springboarded up into my mouth as I scrambled to grab it and check the caller ID. I didn't recognize the wireless number displayed there. All I recognized was the fact that it was not Daniel.

"Hello?" I said.

"Annisa? It's Sage."

Huh. Apparently there *was* a first time for everything.

"Sage?"

"Yeah. Can you get a ride over here?" she asked. She sounded tense. Tense and wired and conspiratorial. I sat up straight and put my feet flat on the floor. My mischief radar hummed forebodingly.

"What?"

Sage grumbled in the back of her throat. "Can you get a ride over here?" she repeated impatiently. "To my house? Like, now?"

I blinked and looked around my room, figuring I'd see an oversized penguin sitting in my bed or Mickey Mouse playing cards with my third-grade teacher. Both recurring and freakish dreams I'd been having since I was about eight.

I saw nothing but my messy bedspread and half the contents of my closet strewn across the floor. Total normalcy.

"I guess. Why?" I asked.

"I'm calling a meeting," Sage said. "I have an idea of what we can do about the guys."

Okay. This was making no sense whatsoever. I pinched my arm and then gasped for breath as tears stung my eyes. Smart move.

"What we can do about the guys?" I asked.

"You know. For what they did with the props box," Sage said. "It's called revenge?" she added. "I believe people from *Joisey* know something about the concept."

Great. More mobster jokes. Like I hadn't heard fourteen thousand of those since I'd moved here. Thank you, HBO.

But wait. Was she serious? Sage Barnard, Flirt Addict Numero Uno, wanted to get back at the guys? Sheesh. Apparently these people really *did* take their props box seriously. Which just made it all the more irritating that no one had freaked out when someone had thrown in the highly inappropriate suggestion of dyeing my hair.

Okay. Bygones. I was over that. Really.

"But you *like* the guys," I said, thoroughly confused.

Sage clucked her tongue with obvious impatience. In the background I heard a doorbell ring and a bevy of familiar voices greet each other.

"Will you just get over here? Everyone's either here already or on their way," Sage said.

Figures she would have called me last. "I'll be there in ten minutes." The line went dead before I even had a chance to say good-bye.

Unfortunately, my parents were not, in fact, home. They

had to go to some black-tie event at the upscale department store where my mother worked as a personal shopper. (In other words, my father was in his own personal hell.) There was only one other option if I didn't want to be left out of this latest squad meeting. One neither of my parents would have liked.

I got up, walked down the hall and knocked on my brother's door. He swung it open two seconds later.

"What's up?" he asked. On the floor of his room were stacks of books and CDs. The kid was *organizing*. His break needed to end soon or he was going to lose it. Lucky for him he was headed back to class on Monday. And, I'm sure my parents were hoping, another brand-new makeover.

"Bored?" I asked.

"You have no idea," he replied.

"That motorcycle of yours have a passenger's helmet?" I asked.

Gabe's eyes went wide. "You want a ride?"

"Just call me Biker Babe," I said.

"Whoo-hoo!" Gabe shouted, grabbing his leather jacket and slamming his bedroom door as he emerged into the hall. "Let's roll!"

• • •

By the time I got to Sage's house, I was a total Harley hussy. That thing was *awesome*. It was so cool, leaning into turns, the wind in my . . . well . . . face. (All my hair was tucked under the helmet.) And my brother wasn't kidding. He *was* a responsible rider. I wished my dad would cave in and go for a ride with him already. Then maybe he could stop worrying about Gabe. And, you know, let me ride with him.

"Now remember, if anyone asks how I got over here, I carpooled," I said as I lifted off the helmet.

"You got it," Gabe replied. He reached out his hand and I slapped it, but instead of letting go, he grabbed my fingers up and moved them through an increasingly intricate handshake that ended with a fist pound.

"Right on," I joked.

Gabe rolled his eyes and I jogged to the front door as he revved up and roared off.

"Finally!" Sage said, whipping open the door before I could even ring the bell.

"Good to see you too, Sage," I replied.

"Come on. Everyone's waiting."

She led the way into the living room, calling out to everyone that I had arrived and we could start. As soon as all the squad members—the female ones only, of course—were gathered in her white-on-white living room, Sage dimmed the recessed lights and stood up in front of us. Apparently, she really was serious about this revenge plan of hers. Deadly serious. Her attitude had even affected her fashion choices. Her hair was flattened and hung long and straight down her back, and she wore a no-nonsense black turtleneck. I had never seen Sage wear black before in my life.

"What is this?" Chandra asked, pulling her foot up on the couch. "Are we having a meeting or are you putting on some kind of play?"

A few people giggled.

"Feet off the furniture!" Sage snapped.

Instantly, Chandra's sneaker hit the wood floor.

"Her mom is kind of a freak about stains," Phoebe whispered.

I gulped. No wonder neither Sage nor Whitney had ever held a squad gathering before. The place *was* like a museum with all its glass cases full of vases and artifacts, strategic lighting and white walls. It must have been torture growing up in a place like this. When I was six, I had drawn a mural for my parents on the dining room wall with indelible ink. After an initial screech of shock from my mom, my parents had decided to leave it there as a conversation piece and had actually shown off about my creativity to their friends. I kind of had a feeling markers were verboten in this house. And Play-Doh and fruit punch. Pretty much anything with a color.

"Now, the reason I have called you all here is because of the shocking events of this afternoon," Sage said, standing before us with her hands behind her back. "The men on our squad took what was once a beautiful tradition and made a mockery of it."

A beautiful tradition? Had everyone forgotten that the first-ever SDH props box had been cracked open just *last* season? Apparently. Because angry murmurs filled the room. I felt like I was at some kind of union meeting. Were we going to form a protest or something?

"All they have done since joining our squad is disrupt it," Sage continued.

"Talk about jumping ship," Chandra whispered. "I just got splashed."

I covered my mouth to keep from laughing. It seemed that if Sage was going to switch sides, she was going to do so full-force. And apparently no one was going to question her conversion. I think everyone was too livid at the guys to really care.

"And it is my feeling that we can no longer tolerate such behavior. We have to teach these guys a lesson," Sage said, her blue eyes glinting. "And I have a plan."

Tara sat forward in her seat in eager anticipation. I swear I heard several people panting. We waited for Sage's evil mind to reveal its blackest depths. And waited. And waited.

"Well?" Tara said finally.

Sage slowly smiled, savoring her moment as the center of our tiny little universe.

"Wednesday afternoon is the pep rally for the West Wind rivalry games," Sage said. "I suggest that if the guys think they're so cool and fabulous, that we let them have it."

There was a moment of silence.

"Have what?" I said finally.

Sage rolled her eyes in impatience, like I was sporting an IQ of ten. But to be honest, I don't think anyone else in the room got it either. So who was the low-IQ chica here, I ask you?

"The pep rally!" Sage said, spreading her arms wide. "Let them get out there and try to run the thing on their own. They think cheerleading is so easy and mockable? They think they're so freakin' great? Let them show the whole school!"

I felt a thrill of excitement sprout up in my chest. Talk about an ego check. Terrell, Daniel, Joe and Steven would have no idea what to do out there without us. This would totally show them how difficult cheerleading really was—that we're not just a bunch of silly girls with no brains. Sage really *was* an evil genius.

"Oh, this is perfect!" Jaimee said, clasping her hands together. "They won't know what hit them!"

"They're gonna be totally humiliated," Tara said gleefully. "I love it."

And then, I felt a little squeeze of doubt. They *would* be totally humiliated. The entire school would be watching as they fumbled and stumbled and were completely confused. And as a person who had humiliated herself publicly on more than one occasion, I knew how horrible that felt. Was that really a fair punishment?

"They deserve it after everything they've done," Chandra said in my ear, sounding very much like my shoulder devil. All around us people schemed and planned and laughed. "Don't go soft on us now."

"What are you, a mind-reader?" I asked, startled.

"It's written all over your face," Chandra told me. "I know he's your boyfriend, but do you think he had you in mind when he crashed our party and let Terrell take all those awful pictures? No. We have to get them back."

Damn. Chandra would make a *fab* shoulder devil. Because she was right. After everything, the guys really did need a wake-up call. They couldn't continue to disrespect us and everything we cared about and get away with it. And public humiliation would definitely be a fine wake-up call.

Besides, it wasn't like *I* was doing something to *Daniel*. It was all of us, together, teaching all of *them* a lesson. And if I wanted to further rationalize it (which I did), Daniel had been avoiding me for the last forty-eight hours—averting his eyes, walking away from me in the hall. I was pretty sure he didn't even want to be my boyfriend anymore and yet he was keeping me hanging. He didn't even have the decency to *tell* me. So what exactly did I want to protect him for?

"So? Whaddaya say?" Chandra asked.

I say . . . I say . . .

"I'm in," I told her with a resolute nod.

"Yes!" She wrapped her arm around me and gave me a squeeze.

Too bad I wasn't quite as excited as she was. Even though part of me knew the guys deserved what they had coming to them, I knew it was going to take every ounce of self-control I had in me not to warn Daniel, and not to die of overwhelming guilt in the process.

• • •

When Bethany opened the door on Wednesday morning to find me standing in front of her in my blue, yellow and white uniform, she looked like she might throw up.

"Hi!" I said, waving my dance pom.

"Okay. It's too early for this," she said. Already the door was swinging in toward my face.

"Wait! I'm having a crisis of conscience!" I said, stopping the door with my pom. It got a little crushed, but nothing unfixable.

"And you came to me?" Bethany asked, then laughed. "Interesting choice."

She waved her hand to invite me in, then trudged through her gorgeous, high-ceilinged living room to the breakfast bar in the kitchen, where she was working on an overflowing bowl of chocolate Lucky Charms. Upstairs, hard rock music blared and heavy footsteps pounded around, shaking the chrome pots that hung from the rack above the center island. Her brother Bobby was definitely a big guy.

"Want some?" she asked, shoving a spoonful into her mouth. Milk dribbled from the corners of her lips.

"No, thanks. I'm good," I said. "So, listen, the squad is planning on boycotting the pep rally today."

Bethany dropped her spoon. "Oh, come on!" she said, upset. "You guys are good for one thing—*one thing*—and you can't even give me that!?"

My forehead crinkled in confusion. "I thought you'd be happy. You once said that going to pep rallies was like sliding naked down a sandpaper waterslide into a vat of lemon juice."

Bethany smirked at her old joke, but then her face dropped. "Yeah, that was before it was getting me out of my oral report eighth period," she said.

"Oh. Well, don't worry. We're still gonna have a pep rally," I said. "The idea is to make the guys go out there alone and try to cheer."

"Omigod, you're kidding," she said. "Whose idea was that? It's *brilliant!*"

"Sage's," I said morosely.

Bethany grimaced. "Ugh. Why am I not surprised?" She wiped her mouth with her sleeve and pushed away from the counter.

"Wait! Where're you going?" I asked.

"To get my video camera," she replied. "There's no way I'm missing this."

I sighed, my shoulders slumping. "Hello? Crisis of conscience, remember?"

"Oh. Right," Bethany said. She turned to me and fixed me with a studious expression. "Okay. Hit me."

"The question is whether or not I should warn Daniel," I said.

"No," Bethany answered automatically. "Are we done here?"

"No!" I cried, grabbing her arm as she turned to go again. "That's it? Just no? You don't even want to think about it?"

"I don't *need* to think about it," Bethany said, throwing her hands up. "First of all, you and Daniel aren't even talking and you don't even know if he wants to go out with you anymore, right?"

Wow. Hit a girl where it hurts, why don't you? Of course this was exactly the argument I had been repeating to myself for the last two nights, so why *did* it still hurt?

"Right . . . ," I said slowly.

"Second, if you warn him, he's going to tell the other guys and then all the blah-rahs are going to be mad at you for foiling their devious little plan, right?" she said. "And Athena knows you don't want *that* to happen, right?"

"Right . . ."

"And third, if you tell him, I will miss out on what is quite possibly going to be the most hilarious piece of film ever to be caught on tape. Which, by the way, you cannot do to me," she said. "So the question is, where exactly do your loyalties lie? With me—your bestest best friend—and your blah-rahs, or with a guy who may or may not want to break up with you?"

The very fact that Bethany and the squad were on the same side in something was enough to make a girl's head spin. But somehow, I managed to focus.

"Well, when you put it that way," I said, deflated.

"Great!" Bethany replied, all smiles. "I'll go get my camera and then Me-Bobby-You-Jane and I will drive you to school."

She turned and took the stairs two at a time. "Bobby! Quit flirting with yourself in the mirror and get down here!" she shouted as she went. "We *have* to get to school. This is going to be a very good day . . . ," she sang.

I plopped down on one of the breakfast bar stools and halfheartedly shook a couple of marshmallows out of the Lucky Charms box. Above my head the rock music died and I heard Bethany snickering to herself. Well, at least I'd made *someone* happy.

• • •

"I can't believe we're doing this. Are we really doing this?" Jaimee asked, clasping and unclasping her hands.

"Yes. We're actually doing this," Chandra said, popping her gum as she filed her fingernails. "Chill out already."

"She's right. You need to get more oxygen or you're going to hyperventilate," Autumn told her, standing up from the bench in the locker room. "Breathe with me. In . . . two . . . three. Out . . . two . . . three."

Jaimee did as she was told and I found myself breathing along with her. I was so nervous, I felt like I was about to be shoved out onstage for the school musical without a script. But in reality, I wasn't about to do anything. All I was about to do was sit *behind* the scenes.

And let Daniel, Steven, Joe and Terrell take the fall. Two of whom I liked very much. Or three of whom. Or one and a half of whom. It all depended on what mood I was in when you asked me.

Down the hallway, someone opened the door to the gym to peek out. Instantly the din of hundreds of excited voices filled the locker room. My heart kicked it up another notch. The gym was already filling up. What was going to happen when the cheerleaders didn't show up? Exactly how much trouble were we about to be in?

The noise muted and Tara and Phoebe came scurrying into the room. "Coach Holmes is coming," Tara said. "Everyone just stay calm."

We all snapped to attention. Even Chandra dropped the blasé act. Jaimee reached out and grabbed my hand as the door opened and closed and Coach Holmes finally strode into the room. Time stopped as she took us in. All eighteen of us, alternates included, standing there in our street clothes.

"Where are your uniforms?" she asked. "You were wearing your uniforms when you came in here."

Everyone looked at Sage. Mastermind of our plan. It appeared she was trying to shrink herself down to Bratz size by sheer force of will. Figures. She could talk the talk, but apparently there would be no walking the walk.

"Anyone going to tell me what's going on here?" Coach asked. There was the vein again.

Tara, bless her brave little soul, stepped forward. "We're not going out there," she said.

"What!?" Coach Holmes blurted.

"We think it's about time the guys on the squad found out what it really means to be a cheerleader," Tara said gamely. She wasn't totally cucumber cool, though. Her dangly earring was shaking.

"Tell me you're kidding," Coach said. She looked around at all of us. "Someone tell me you're kidding."

There was no response. A few heads hung in shame. I, myself, was already staring at the laces on my black shoes.

Don't cave, the shoulder angel said. Or was it the devil?

It was getting harder and harder to tell them apart. *They deserve this. Don't cave!*

"You think *this* is going to teach them what it means to be a cheerleader?" Coach asked. "Turning your back on your teammates?"

A lump formed in the back of my throat. She had a point there. This wasn't good sportsmanship. This wasn't being part of a team or rising above anything. This was about plain vindictiveness.

"You guys," I said. "Maybe we should—"

"No." Sage finally spoke up. Probably solely to contradict me. "This was what we all agreed to do. We're sticking to the plan." She turned to Coach Holmes. "Sorry, Coach, but they need to be taught a lesson."

Coach Holmes stared back at Sage, her face set like a stone. For a long moment no one moved and I was fairly certain that Coach was going to demand that we all get our asses out there under penalty of death. Or at least under threat of being thrown off the squad.

Finally, she shook her head. "I hope you girls know what you're doing," she said. Then she turned around and walked out.

The entire squad let out a collective sigh of relief. Coach Holmes had not burst into a ball of flame and incinerated all of us and the entire known universe. The worst was over.

Now all we had to do was wait.

Fifteen minutes later I was experiencing a full-on case of plotter's remorse. I felt sick. Sick and mean and hot and guilty. All I wanted to do was go home and crawl into my bed and pull the covers up over my head. We could hear the confusion in the gym. The murmurs, the laughter. The guys must have been sitting out there on the bottom bleacher by now, alone in their uniforms, wondering where the heck we all were while everyone speculated and salivated. Everything had taken on a level of tension that no pep rally should ever convey. Every moment I kept waiting for the door to open and for Coach Holmes to storm back in and drag us out there. Or for Principal Buzzkill to pound on the door and threaten us with suspensions. But nothing happened, and soon enough, we all heard the president of the student council, senior and bleach blonde Dori Reisfeld, take the microphone.

"Welcome, everyone, to the first winter pep rally of the season!" she shouted, earning a cheer from the crowd.

I could imagine her out there in her blue SDH sweatshirt, her choppy hair sticking out in all directions, her hip-deep dimples widening with her smile. I wondered if she realized what was going on yet. If she would sound quite that chipper if she did.

"Come on. We're going out there," Tara said.

"We are?!" I asked, perking up considerably.

"Not *out there* out there," Tara said, rolling her eyes. "This way."

She waved at us to follow her and walked down the opposite hall to the door that led to the gym lobby. A couple of people exchanged wary glances, but everyone followed. I couldn't believe this. They were actually going out there to *watch*? How sadistic were my teammates?

"You coming?" Jaimee asked, hesitating near the end of the hallway.

I looked around at the empty locker room and a skitter of fear shot through me. I didn't want to be anywhere alone just then, just in case of, you know, angry mobs out for cheerleader blood. There was strength in numbers. I pushed myself up and we walked out together.

The entire squad was already huddled around the six small windows set high in the wooden doors to the gym. I stepped up tentatively behind them, not at all sure I wanted to see any of this.

"Look at Terrell's face!" Tara hissed happily. "He looks like he soiled his pants."

Laughter all around. A couple of the girls even slapped hands. If the guys were where I imagined them to be, that meant that the girls had a full, panoramic view of the guys' misery. I wondered what Daniel was feeling just then.

Probably seething, murderous rage. Directed at me. Any second now *I* might be soiling *my* pants.

"What're we gonna do tonight?" Dori shouted.

"Beat West Wind!" the crowd replied.

"What?" she shouted.

"Beat West Wind!" the cry came back, with some stomping and clapping added.

"Say it again!?"

"Beat West Wind!" The volume was overwhelming.

"You know it!" Dori shouted into the microphone. "So now let's get things started right!" she announced. "Without further delay, I present to you your mighty, fighting Sand Dune Crab cheerleaders!"

The whole place went berserk and I found myself irrevocably drawn to the one tiny corner of window that was left. I shoved myself under Felice's arm and closed my left eye to better see with my right. Inside the gym, the cheers were dying a slow death as Daniel, Terrell, Steven and Joe all got up and awkwardly made their way to the center of the floor.

Dori put her hand over the microphone and whispered something to Coach Holmes. Coach shook her head. On the court, Daniel and Terrell argued under their breath. We couldn't hear them from behind closed doors, but their body language was Desperate with a capital D.

Coach Rincon, whom we hadn't seen in days, pushed himself away from the wall and grabbed Coach Holmes' hand. He said something in her ear and they started conversing, their heads bent together. They both looked seriously mad.

"Do something!" I saw Daniel hiss.

Terrell raised his hands in surrender, like *Don't look at me.* I half expected him to display some of that roadrunner speed of his and bolt from the room, leaving a few scorch marks in the gym floor.

A few of the girls around me giggled. I felt like crying.

"Apparently Terrell isn't such the fearless leader now," Phoebe said.

Everyone in the stands stared. The whispers grew louder and louder. Across the gym, Principal Buzzkill was on the move, making a beeline for our coaches. He was red with rage. Someone had to do something. Fast.

Go in there, my shoulder angel prodded me. *Go save them.* But how? What was I supposed to do dressed in my street clothes and all alone? There was nothing.

And then it happened. Daniel finally started clapping a steady beat, looking around uncertainly. "Go! Hey, here we go! Crabs! Go!" he shouted.

One lonely voice.

Steven hung his head, covering his eyes with both hands. Daniel backed up and whacked Steven's arm with the back of his hand.

"Go! Hey, here we go! Crabs! Go!" Daniel shouted again. He raised a fist in the air on "Go!" Everyone in the stands stared in silence.

I found myself cheering him on silently. *Yeah, you can do it! Get the crowd into it, Daniel. Come on!*

Terrell, meanwhile, shook his head. For a guy who pretty much oozed pride, this dude gave up *way* too easily.

"Yeah, that's right. No idea what to do with yourself without your stunting partner, huh?" Sage said.

Some people were taking a little bit too much joy in their supposed friends' misery.

"Go! Hey, here we go! Crabs! Go!" Daniel shouted again. His voice cracked with nerves and a few people in the stands laughed. We were evil. Pure, unadulterated evil.

"This is sick. I can't watch this," I said, pushing back through the crowd.

"Me neither," Autumn said, joining me.

"We could really use that space-time continuum thing now, huh?" I asked her.

"Definitely."

Suddenly everyone backed up. The doors were flung open and out stormed Coach Rincon. There were little flames where his pupils should have been, I swear. Coach Holmes was hot on his heels.

"What the hell do you girls think you're doing?" he said through his teeth. "How could you do this to your teammates?"

"Leo!" Coach Holmes scolded, looking desperate.

"Why are you doing this?" Rincon asked, shoving his hands under his biceps. "What did they do to you?"

"Th-they crashed our slumber party," Sage said timidly. "And then they—"

"That? Big deal!" Rincon said with a scoff. "That was just a little harmless fun. Boys being boys."

"Wait a minute," Coach Holmes said, approaching him. "You *knew* about this?"

His forehead wrinkled. "Knew about it? I told them to do it."

"What?" about ten of us said in unison.

"What? Daniel and Terrell called me to talk and . . . I thought it would help!" Rincon replied. He turned to Coach Holmes. "Remember that year we went to the final four and no one was speaking? Remember how much fun we had together on that trip?"

"Leo, that was totally different," Coach Holmes said. "I can't believe you told a bunch of teenage boys to crash a teenage girls' slumber party!"

He blinked. Apparently the "teenage" part hadn't

occurred to him before. "Well, did *you* tell *them* to do this?" he said, whirling on her.

"Of course not!"

"But you're condoning it," he said.

"Well, what do you want me to do? Shove them out there?" she asked.

"I want you to get control of your squad!" he replied.

Whoa. Smack all of us in the face, why don't you? Coach Holmes stood up straight. She leveled him with a glare that could have brought whole cities to their knees.

"Are you really going to speak to me like that?" she asked, quaking.

"I don't exactly have a choice," he replied.

"Then get out," she said. "Get out of my school, get away from my squad and get away from me," she said calmly.

In the gym lobby there was complete silence. Out on the gym floor, Terrell and the others had finally, *finally* joined Daniel, but they sounded pathetic. "Go! Hey, here we go! Crabs! Go!"

A couple of people in the stands responded with a lame "Go!" but everyone else just laughed. My heart twisted tighter and tighter and tighter inside my chest until, moments later, it mercifully stopped.

"You really want to do this, Dee?" Rincon said.

"Just go," she said weakly.

"Fine," he said. Then he turned and stormed out, letting the door slam behind him.

"Uh . . . your mighty, fighting Sand Dune Crab cheerleaders!" Dori said into the microphone, her nervous laugh echoing throughout the gym. "Let's hear it for them!"

We all looked at each other with dread as Coach Holmes stood there, catatonic.

A wave of lackluster applause trickled through the crowd in the gym and I closed my eyes against the humiliated and sad tears that threatened to overflow. I wasn't even humiliated for the guys. I was humiliated for myself. How could I have thought this was a good idea? The guys were miserable, our coaches were miserable, we were all miserable. Didn't get much worse than that.

"Thanks a lot, ladies," Coach said, looking around at us. She ducked her head and walked back into the gym as if she were walking to meet her executioner.

"Well. That was the most pep-free rally in history," Tara said.

I turned around and headed for the nearest bathroom stall.

• • •

"That can't be a good sign," Chandra said when we walked into the auditorium that afternoon after school.

We had found a note taped to the locker room door telling us all not to get changed and to meet here instead of at one of our practice locales. One look at Coach Holmes' Unibomber scrawl and already we knew we were in serious trouble. When we saw Principal Buzzkill standing near the stage with Coach, their heads bent in conversation, we knew we were dead for sure. My legs turned to jelly as we walked down the center aisle. All four guys sat in the front row on the left side, facing resolutely forward. On the opposite side of the aisle, Jaimee and Autumn turned around in their seats, eyes wide, like lambs about to be sent to the slaughter.

"What's he doing here?" Tara hissed, coming up behind us.

"My guess is, it's not to offer us school spirit awards," I told her.

I dropped into a seat near the center of the second row and gradually all the chairs around me filled in. Autumn sat in front of me, her fingertips and thumbs pressed together and turned toward the rafters as she tried to meditate. Chandra unwrapped a huge Snickers bar and chomped down on it. Tara's pen tapped against her notebook at a frightening speed.

"All right. Now that everyone's here, your principal would like to say a few words," Coach Holmes announced.

Principal Buzzkill cleared his throat and stepped forward. He held one arm across his chest and crooked the other so that his fist was covering his mouth, like a man in mourning. His pose was that serious and contemplative. His blond hair glinted under the auditorium lights, which also highlighted his tan skin and handsome features. A man that good-looking was never meant to be a principal. Especially not such a strict, scary one.

The anticipation of a lecture is never fun. It's even worse when you know you deserve it. Maybe if I admitted that I was wrong, he'd let me leave.

Yeah. And maybe tomorrow he'd take us on a free field trip to Universal Studios.

I took out a red pen and started drawing swirls on the cover of my history notebook. Anything to keep from mistakenly looking him in the eye.

"What happened this afternoon was unacceptable," Principal Buzzkill began. As usual, the man pulled no punches. Right to the point, like an arrow to a bull's-eye. "Pep rallies are an important component of student life at this school. They are meant to engender school spirit and pride. What you people pulled today undermined everything that event stands for. Now, your coach has been trying to explain to me the reasoning behind your actions, and as far as I'm concerned, those reasons are unacceptable. As cheerleaders, your first responsibility is to this school, not to your own petty arguments."

The longer he spoke, the further my head bowed. My skin felt like someone had lit a Bunsen burner beneath it. My pen dug deeper and deeper into my notebook cover with each new swirl.

"Now, I need to meet with the vice principal and the director of athletics to decide what, if any, punishment we'll hand down for this sorry display," Buzzkill continued. "But let me just leave you with this one thought. Pep rallies are a privilege, not a right. And privileges can easily be revoked."

No. No way. My head snapped up at this and, of course, I looked right into his cold, dead eyes. The man didn't so much as flinch. I glanced at Tara, who looked like someone had just told her Paul Mitchell was discontinuing her favorite line of hair care products. Damn, Buzzkill was good. He knew exactly where and how hard to twist the screws. I mean, taking away our pep rallies? Why not just drive a stake into our hearts already?

"Coach Holmes? They're all yours," he said.

Then he walked out, head held high like a man who'd just severely beaten down the enemy.

"He can't do that, can he?" Tara said as soon as the door was closed. "We have to have pep rallies."

"Like you care," Terrell said.

"Yeah, we didn't exactly have one today," Daniel said. "And whose fault is that?"

"Yours," Sage replied vehemently. "If you hadn't been such total a—"

"That's enough!" Coach shouted, silencing everyone.

For the first time I realized how unlike herself she looked. Normally the most powerful woman in any room, Coach now looked small and skinny and wan. Her cheeks were slightly sunken and her eyes were tired and makeup-free. Weird. I could have sworn she'd been wearing her usual liner and shadow earlier, which meant that either she had taken it off between the pep rally and now or . . . or she'd been crying.

Gulp. Apparently these arguments between her and Rincon were pretty serious.

Coach Holmes took a deep breath and ran both hands over her face. I exchanged a disturbed glance with Chandra. This was not the Coach we knew and loved and sort of feared. This was someone else entirely.

"Okay, listen, I am willing to admit that I made a mistake here," she said finally.

Double gulp. Seriously?

"I should have never opened up the tryouts to guys because *clearly* this group is not yet mature enough to handle a coed existence," she said, staring us down.

Zing. Okay. There was a little bit of her left in there.

"But we have a bit of a problem," she continued, crossing

her arms over her chest. "This school needs a cheerleading squad, so as much as I might like to after today's debacle, I can't disband the team."

Um . . . ouch!

"But I also can't throw the guys off the squad, *or* the girls, without a lawsuit," she continued. "So here we are," she said, throwing her arms wide and then letting them slap down. "We are stuck together. And I am out of ideas."

I glanced across the aisle at the guys. For once they looked as shamed and small as the rest of us did. Daniel's face was blotched with red and Steven was leaning his elbow on the armrest, holding his hand over his mouth.

"So I put it to you," Coach said finally. She started to gather up her things—her jacket, her bag, her clipboard. "You all need to find a way to fix this and you need to do it fast. Otherwise this season is going to be a total wash." She started up the aisle, then paused right at the end of our row and turned halfway around. Like she couldn't even bear to fully look at us anymore. "I expect to see all of you here tonight at seven for the pregame warm-up. You can give me your solution at that time."

As soon as Coach was gone, the room was filled with sighs, like someone had just let the air out of two dozen balloons. We shifted in our seats. Sage and Karianna whispered to each other. Everyone was waiting for someone else to say something first. But what?

We're sorry? Did anyone other than me want to say that? And even if we did, would the guys care?

"Well?" Terrell said finally, turning in his seat and hooking his arm around the back of the chair.

"Well what?" Tara replied.

"You really got nothing to say," Terrell said. "Nothing at all."

Tara simply sat there and stared straight ahead, shaking her head in disbelief. Could she really not see that the guys deserved an apology?

"We're sorry, all right?" I blurted, standing up.

"Annisa!" Chandra said.

"No! We're not!" Sage put in, whipping around to face me.

"What's wrong with you guys?" I asked, feeling desperate enough to pop. "If someone did to us what we just did to them, you'd be freaking out."

"They need to apologize to us first," Tara told me, standing as well. "That's the way it works."

"Like we're really going to apologize after what you just did to us," Daniel said.

He looked so hurt, I just wanted to go over there and hug him. But there was a giant force field between us, keeping me from moving a muscle.

"Wait a minute, apologize for what?" Terrell asked, incredulous. "What the hell do we need to apologize for?"

Tara let out an indignant laugh-squeal that echoed through the room.

"Uh . . . I don't know . . . for the slumber party, for the props box?" Sage said. "Or how about for your very existence?"

My head fell forward. Sage had just gone one too far.

"That's it. I'm outta here," Daniel said, grabbing his varsity jacket.

He stormed out, slamming into the wooden door so hard, it flew open and crashed back against the outer wall.

Terrell slowly gathered his things, shaking his head and chuckling derisively. "Nice work," he said as he paused in the center aisle. "Hope you girls come up with something good to tell Coach tonight, because I'm gonna have nothing to say."

I swallowed hard and looked around at my friends. Never had I seen so much misery and anger.

"You guys coming?" he asked.

Instantly, Joe and Steven were on their feet. The three of them trudged out together, leaving the rest of us to clean up the mess. Unfortunately, it seemed like there wasn't a cheerleader among us who had a single clue where to start.

Maybe I'm just a glutton for punishment. Or maybe I'm an eternal optimist. Or maybe I just loved the guy. But whatever the reason, after I left school that afternoon, I went directly to Daniel's house, do not pass "Go," do not collect two hundred dollars. I felt so bad for what we'd done to him, I had to try to apologize again. Even if I was still a little bit angry about the slumber party and the props box, what we had done that day had been so much worse. Besides, we had to start somewhere trying to fix this thing.

At least I thought we did. Hopefully he felt the same way.

As I walked up the driveway to his house, I felt so unwelcome, I kept waiting for a pit bull to come running around the side of the house and attack. Or for someone to fire a warning shot from one of the upstairs windows. But neither of those happened and soon enough I was reaching for the doorbell, shaking so much that I actually missed the button and jammed my finger into the wall. I got it on the second try.

Moments later the curtain on the side window was drawn aside and Daniel peeked out. He paused for a moment, then let the curtain drop. I half expected my heart to burst out and fall into my hands. Is that where that expression comes from? *She came with her heart in her hands?*

Kind of gross when you think about it.

It took so long for the door to open, I half thought he'd decided to just leave me there. Not that I could blame him. But then, finally, the doorknob turned.

And I was face-to-face with Daniel's mother. All five-foot-ten of her. I suppose you had to be that big to handle giving birth to, and then raising, four football-playing boys. Daniel was the baby and he was at least six feet tall.

But wait, what was going on here? Did I just hallucinate? Had I or had I not seen Daniel in the window? Had he really sent his mother to get rid of me?

This was not a good sign for the future of our relationship.

"Hi there, hon," Mrs. Healy said. The slight Southern accent left over from her girlhood in Alabama gave her voice a natural soothing quality. She also threw in a sympathetic head tilt. My first real clue that I was getting nowhere near my maybe-boyfriend.

Ugh. My maybe-boyfriend. Again. How had we gone from I-love-yous to maybe-ness in just a few weeks?

"Uh . . . hi," I said, feeling like a clueless idiot. An itty-bitty little clueless idiot who was shrinking smaller by the second. "Is . . . Daniel here?"

"I'm sorry, Annisa, but he doesn't really feel like talkin' right now," she said, in a conciliatory tone that made me think of nurses and hospitals and really bad news. She leaned forward and whispered, "I think he just needs some time to cool off. You know how boys can be."

No. I didn't. Not really. Maybe I should ask her to give me lessons. Having raised four of them, she could be like my guy guru. Teach me, O wise one.

"Uh . . . sure," I said, backing away. "Can you just . . . just tell him I'll see him at the game?" I asked.

"Sure thing, hon," she said with a kind smile. A kind smile that made me think she knew something that I didn't. Like how Daniel was never going to speak to me again.

"Thanks," I said.

Then I turned and ran before I ended up weeping in front of my maybe-boyfriend's mother.

• • •

That night, the squad completely sucked. I mean, we sucked like we had never sucked before. After the first quarter Tara called the "Let's Go" cheer and half the squad started doing a newish cheer we'd learned that started with the words "Let's go" while the other half launched into the classic "Let's Go" cheer. We ended up shouting over one another in a garble of messed-up chants, and stepping on each other's toes as we stumbled through opposing formation changes. Then Lindsey threw up a high V when she should have low-V-ed and punched Karianna right in the face.

Although I'm pretty sure that one was on purpose.

Coach shook her head as we jogged back off the court. "Have you all forgotten this is West Wind?" she whispered, leaning forward in her seat. "Get it together!"

I glanced down the bleachers at our rivals' side and saw their squad snickering and pointing. Was it wrong that I was hoping that particular portion of our gym ceiling might spontaneously cave in?

"It's a little late to be trying to get it together now," Chandra whispered, taking a sip of water from a bottle she kept on the bleacher between her feet.

"Seriously," I replied.

Our pregame meeting with Coach hadn't gone exactly as she'd hoped. When she had asked us what our solution for the team was, no one had said a word. Not even Tara or Terrell. I had just stared down at my pleats until she had finally thrown her hands up and left us to stretch. Notch up one more disappointment on our long belt of disappointments.

Throughout the second quarter, no one felt like cheering. We were supposed to do chants almost continuously, but Coach had to keep whispering Tara's name to get her to call the cheers. The basketball team wasn't helping matters much. They looked like a bunch of amateurs out there, turning the ball over, muffing passes and slamming every potential three-pointer right off the backboard. Meanwhile, the West Wind Dolphins might as well have just stepped off the bus from Shaq camp. Every time they got the ball, it was a swish fest. Three-pointer . . . swish. Layup . . . swish. Flying acrobatic dunk, accompanied by foot to the face of the Sand Dune guard . . . jam, bam, ice pack. By the time the half was over, we were down by twenty points.

"All right, come on, you guys," Tara said as we stood up to take center court for the halftime cheer. "Let's show these people what we can do."

I looked at Daniel as he jumped down to the floor. He did not look at me. Not that I was surprised. All night he had been freezing me out. In fact, the air between us could have probably been chipped up and used for slushies.

And I was supposed to let this person toss me into the air? Somehow I wasn't feeling it.

At least Coach had decided to do a fairly simple cheer at halftime. No huge pyramids, no major throws. Just cupies on the last run-through. One stunt to hit. Apparently she knew how to hedge her bets.

I stood in formation and faced the crowd. It felt like everyone was on the edge of their seats, just waiting for something interesting—anything at all—to happen. Not that I could blame them. After that pep rally, I would have been salivating for more insanity too.

"SDH!" Tara called. "Ready?"

"Okay!

S! D! H!

S! D! H!

Who's the team that's gonna win?"

I crouched down in front of my laminated "H" sign.

"S!"

Phoebe thrust the S over her head.

"D!"

Sage thrust the D over her head.

"H!"

My turn. I thrust the H up.

"Who's the team we're cheering for?"

"S! D! H!" The crowd shouted back at us as we raised our signs again. I smiled. Okay. This was good. Crowd participation. No mess-ups so far. We even sounded pretty loud and energetic.

Maybe all was not lost.

"Who's the team that's gonna win?"

"S! D! H!"

I backed toward Daniel and handed the sign off to Jaimee, who was staying floor bound for this one. Chandra and Autumn took the other signs.

"Come on, say it loud and proud!"

"S!"

Phoebe went up into her cupie . . . then squealed and came right back down. The entire crowd gasped. Joe caught her awkwardly and she shouted in pain, crumpling to the floor as she clutched her ankle. The damage was done. We probably should have stayed on point, but several squad members turned around to look, fearing the worst, and now our timing was all thrown off.

"D!" Tara and a few of the more conscientious cheerleaders shouted.

Sage and Terrell didn't even try their cupie. Coach Holmes' head hung.

"Are we doing this?" Daniel said in my ear.

I just nodded. We had to save the cheer. We had to do something!

"H!" I shouted at the top of my lungs.

I went up and Daniel caught my feet. Solid. I thrust my hands into a high V and grinned. The few people in the stands who hadn't already covered their faces with their hands gaped at me. The only cheerleader still cheering. On the floor, the rest of the squad was in shambles.

And then they started to boo. They actually started to boo. And the longer I was up there, the louder the noise grew.

"Um. I think I should come down now," I said through my forced grin.

"Okay. One, two," Daniel said.

We cradled out and all I wanted to do was curl up into

a ball and cry. But instead, the second I was down, I jumped out of Daniel's arms and ran to check on Phoebe with the rest of the squad.

"Are you okay?" I asked, crouching on the floor as boos and jeers continued to rain down on us.

"Yeah. I think I may have just sprained it," Phoebe said, wincing.

"I can't believe they're booing us," Sage said. "We're national champions. Hello?"

"I think that's *why* they're booing us," Chandra said. "They expect a little more from us than *this.*"

We took it all in, the squad gathered in a clump on the floor. Our signs tossed aside. Poms everywhere. Chandra was right. We were a huge disappointment. After leaving Daniel's house that afternoon, I felt like I had hit my lowest low. Now I knew there was always somewhere lower.

"Hey, Sand Dune!"

We all looked up to see the West Wind High captain sauntering by us with her squad in tow. Their green-and-white uniforms had glittering letters across the front and the captain had worn green glitter eye shadow to match. The overall look was very Wicked Witch of the West.

"Nice routine," the girl said. "Really hot. Did you practice the part where you all fall on your faces or does that just come naturally to you?"

"Back off, Jenna," Tara said.

"Oooh. Or what? You'll sic your men on me?" Jenna said, raising both hands. "Somehow I'm not that concerned," she added, looking the guys over with one eyebrow raised, like they were just so lame. Then she turned on her heel and

walked out into the lobby, taking her band of flying mon-
keys with her.

Like I said. Always somewhere lower.

• • •

Friday night, my mother and I walked out of our house with
our winter jackets on. A cold snap had finally hit Sand Dune
and we had been forced to unpack the coats and gloves. Yes,
gloves. Never thought those things would see the light of day
again. Anyway, it was too cold and too dark for me to walk
to school to catch the fan bus to K.C.'s latest match, so Mom
had offered to drive me. My hand had just reached for the
door handle on her car when a pair of headlights swung into
the driveway.

Honda Civic headlights. Daniel Healy's headlights.

And I was the proverbial deer caught in them.

"Hon?" my mom said, her breath making steam in the
cold air.

"Uh . . . maybe I have a ride?" I said uncertainly.

"Want me to wait inside?" she asked, clutching her coat
closer to her.

Daniel was staring at me through the windshield. I
couldn't read his expression.

"Uh . . . I guess?" I said.

My mother smiled at me encouragingly. "I'm right in
there if you need me," she said. Then she jogged back inside
to enjoy the heat. Which had been turned on for the first
time today. The second she was gone, Daniel got out of the
car. He left it running. For what? So he could make a quick
getaway after he finally, officially broke up with me?

"Hey," he said, pushing his hands into the pockets of his

varsity jacket. He had topped it with a blue scarf, no gloves. Boys. Always trying to be so tough.

"Hey," I said.

"You going to the thing?" he asked.

"Yeah. You?"

"Yeah."

Well. This was a stunningly fascinating conversation.

Daniel took a few steps toward me. "Annisa, I can't take this anymore," he said. "I should never have joined this stupid squad."

"Don't say that," I said.

"No. It's true," he told me, locking his clear blue eyes on mine. "We never fought before this. A couple of weeks ago I couldn't even imagine being mad at you and now—"

"Now you're mad at me all the time," I finished.

Daniel smirked. "Well, not *all* the time."

My shoulder muscles uncoiled. "Daniel, I'm so sorry about the pep rally. I mean, I was all caught up in Sage's plan and I didn't realize exactly how bad it was going to be until, you know, I saw it."

"Yeah. It sucked pretty hard," he said. "But I kind of understand the pack mentality thing. Terrell is *really* good at talking me into stuff. And I don't know why," he said, narrowing his eyes.

I snorted a laugh. "Maybe because he's the devil?"

"Could be," Daniel said.

We stood there for a moment, shivering in silence. This was the most we had said to each other in days. All I wanted to do was hug him. I felt like some invisible force was pushing me toward him, but I held my ground. I still didn't know if *he* wanted to hug *me*. I felt so awkward just standing there.

"So . . . what do we do now?" I said finally.

He looked at me out of the corner of his eye, then stepped even closer. My breath caught and I realized that a big part of me had thought he would never be this close to me again.

"Well, for starters, I was thinking this," he said.

And then he reached out and pulled me into his arms. I pressed my face against the cold leather of his jacket and squeezed my eyes closed. Sweet relief! I felt like I was really breathing for the first time all week.

"What do you think?" he asked lightly.

"This is good!" I replied, my voice cracking.

Daniel leaned back and smiled. "So you don't hate me anymore?"

"I never *hated* you," I replied. "Do you still hate me?"

"I never hated you either," he said.

Big sigh.

"I thought you were never going to talk to me again," I said. "I came to your house . . ." I trailed off. We both knew I'd come to his house. We both knew that I knew that he'd seen me. How had things gotten so complicated?

"I'm sorry about the freeze-out," Daniel said. "I just needed some time to chill. If I'd talked to you that day . . ."

Now it was his turn to let the sentence hang. I swallowed hard, realizing how he would have finished it. *If I'd talked to you that day . . . we would have broken up.*

This really hurt. No one ever told you how much having a boyfriend could *really hurt.* Two days ago, Daniel had seriously thought about breaking up with me. I could hardly believe it.

"Anyway, there's still something you have to explain," Daniel said.

He let me go and took a couple steps back. My stomach dropped. The chili I had eaten for dinner gurgled. Mental note: Chili is never a good idea in the midst of relationship uncertainty.

"What?" I asked, shivering from both the cold and the abject fear.

"I guess I still don't understand why you were so mad at me," he said.

Oh, yeah. That. How to explain? I tilted my head back to look at him and gave it my best shot.

"I think I just felt like . . . like you were choosing the guys over me," I said. "Like it was more important to you to . . . I don't know, make Terrell laugh than to think about me. My feelings."

Daniel blew out a sigh. "I guess I said some mean things at the slumber party, huh?"

"Yeah. Kind of. But it wasn't just that. I told you how important that night was to all of us and it was like you just ignored it," I said.

"I didn't ignore it," Daniel said. "I just didn't get it."

"Well, maybe that's the problem. It doesn't matter if you *get* it. You just have to . . . I don't know . . ."

"Respect it? Listen better?" Daniel offered.

I smirked. "Maybe. Have you been going to therapy or something?"

"Nah. Just talked to Steven about it," Daniel said with a smile. "Did you know his parents are psychologists?"

"That's right!" I said. "I forgot he's good at this stuff."

"Well, all right. I'll try to be better, but then the same goes for you," Daniel said. "You have to listen better to me."

"When have I not listened?" I asked, baffled.

Daniel laughed. "Oh, I don't know, every time I've told you that something was a joke? You take everything so seriously, Annisa, and sometimes I really *am* just kidding."

My heart turned and I looked at the ground, embarrassed. I guess if I expected Daniel to eat a little crow, I would have to do some chewing myself. After all, I *knew* I wasn't totally in the right. I guess it was just sort of difficult to hear it.

"You think you could do that? Not take stuff so seriously?" he said, ducking his head to try to catch my eye. There was a big lump in my throat, but I knew I had to answer him.

"I guess so," I said, rolling my eyes comically.

Daniel grinned and my heart completely unclenched for the first time in days.

"Good," he said. Then he took a deep breath and blew it out. "Whew. This couple thing is hard," he joked.

"Tell me about it," I said with a smile.

"So we're cool?" he asked.

The smile widened as relief flooded through me. We were not breaking up. We were making up! Right here, right now. "Yeah. We're cool."

"Good. So . . . you wanna go to school before they all leave without us?" he said, turning one shoulder toward the car.

"Wait! Don't you want to do the whole best-part-of-fighting thing?" I said, jumping forward. I was giddy. I couldn't help it.

Daniel looked adorably confused. "What's that? Oh, man. Is that something you've told me that I didn't listen to?"

"Ha-ha," I said, shoving his shoulder. "No, no, no. It's kissing and making up."

"Oh! Right! That!" Daniel looked happier than I'd seen him in a long time. "Now *that* I can handle."

And then I kissed him, and he kissed me back, and we stayed there for I don't know how long, just keeping each other warm.

We were late. Guess make-up smooching can kind of make a person lose track of time. The two fan buses were still idling at the curb in front of the school when Daniel and I pulled up, but it seemed like they were all loaded up and ready to go. Daniel killed the engine and grabbed my hand as we made a run for it. As soon as his fingers touched mine, I didn't much care whether we made it to the wrestling match or not. Daniel was holding my hand again. This night could not get any better.

As we raced around the side of the bus, I saw Tara, Phoebe and Sage staring at me through the windows toward the back. They did not look happy. They looked, in fact, thoroughly betrayed. Like I was holding hands with the enemy.

Gulp.

Somehow I had forgotten that the squad was still in a boy-vs.-girl clash to the death. Somehow making up with Daniel had blocked out everything else. But now we were about to enter the ring, together. On that bus was half the squad. How would they feel about me and Daniel making nice?

I was completely out of breath, more from a bizarre concoction of nerves and excitement than from the short sprint, when we got to the door of the bus. A couple of parentals from the PTA booster club stood outside the door and welcomed us on. They wore blue-and-yellow ribbons on their lapels and one of them was sporting a blue foam hat shaped like a crab, which looked like it had seen better days.

"You just made it!" Crab-Lady said with a pearly white smile. She stepped back to let us through.

"Thanks," I said as Daniel let me board ahead of him.

We stepped up onto the bus and Daniel put his hands on my shoulders from behind as I walked down the aisle. I might as well have been wearing a target on my forehead. Interspersed throughout the regular old fans were our various teammates, and if looks could kill, we would have died ten times over. There were Terrell and Joe, glaring at Daniel's hands like they would have liked to amputate them. There were Lindsey and Karianna, jaws dropped in such indignation, you would have thought I was wearing West Wind colors. Sage blew out a noisy sigh through her lips and Tara Timothy shook her head in disgust.

"I think it's colder in here than it is outside," Daniel joked in my ear.

I cracked a smile. He got it in one. About the only person that seemed happy to see us touching was Mindy, who waved at us from a three-seater at the center of the bus.

I really missed having Mindy on the squad. Always the voice of reason. The basketball team was lucky to have her.

"You guys made up?" she said with a grin.

"Yep. Just now," I said, dropping into the seat next to her.

Daniel mushed in, letting one of his knees jut out into the aisle. I slumped down so far, my jacket rode up my back and my knees pressed into the seat in front of me. Daniel and Mindy both looked down at me, their blue eyes concerned. For the first time, I realized how similar they looked. Blond-haired, blue-eyed gorgeousness. They could be twins. Disturbing.

"Uh, Annisa?" Daniel asked. "What're you doing?"

"Hiding," I told him.

"Why?" Mindy asked.

"Have you not noticed that the entire cheerleading squad wants us dead?" I whispered as the bus roared to life. "We're traitors. We're Romeo and Juliet and they're the Capulets and Montagues."

Mindy laughed. "Don't be so dramatic." Then she got up on her knees and looked around. Instantly her face fell and she sank back down again, hunkering a bit lower than before. "Okay. I get your point."

Apparently, she'd been hit by a few death rays by association.

Daniel reached out and laced his fingers through mine. "So they're staring. So what?" he said. "I'm not going to let this squad affect us anymore."

"No?" I said, perking up slightly.

"I know you want the squad to be important to me, and it is," he said. "But not as important as us."

I grinned and sat up a bit. "Really?"

"Yeah. And as far as I'm concerned, they can all kiss my big old male-cheerleader butt!" Daniel shouted.

A bunch of people around us laughed and I pushed myself completely straight in my seat. Daniel was right. We couldn't let them affect our relationship. If we as a couple were stronger than the squad, then so be it. I shouldn't be ashamed of it.

"Hey! Maybe if you guys can get back together, there's still hope for the squad," Mindy said optimistically.

"Maybe . . . ," I said.

I pushed myself up and glanced back over the seat at Tara and Phoebe, who were grumbling to each other and glaring over at us every few seconds. A chill shot through me and I dropped back down, cuddling closer to Daniel for warmth. Suddenly a spirit pom came flying from the direction of Terrell and Joe's seat and smacked Daniel in the head. His jaw clenched, but he ignored it and let it slide to the floor.

"Or maybe not."

This was going to be one interesting wrestling match. I just hoped none of the cheerleaders ended up out on the mats.

• • •

"This isn't happening," Jaimee whispered, rocking forward and back behind me. "This isn't happening, this isn't happening. . . ."

Down on the mat, the ref called the end of the first two-minute period. K.C. got up off the floor, winded and extremely confused. His opponent clapped his hands together and shouted in triumph as he went for his water bottle. I narrowed my eyes at him in irritation. This guy was beating K.C. He was actually *beating* K.C.

"Who does this guy think he is, the Rock?" Chandra said.

Actually, if this kid was looking for a Hollywood career, he definitely could have doubled for the Rock. He was absolutely tremendous. His muscles bulged like Wolverine's and he had about the same bloodthirsty attitude. Somehow

K.C. had avoided getting pinned and automatically losing, but I could not figure out how. Wolverine had already racked up so many points with takedowns and reversals, I'd lost count. Meanwhile, K.C. hadn't scored one. Not a single point.

"It's like his concentration is totally shot," Daniel said.

Everyone around me pointedly ignored him. The girls on the squad had actually deigned to sit near us, but hadn't acknowledged his existence all night. It was kind of irritating, but I figured they'd get used to him again. Eventually.

"Weigh him again, ref!" someone shouted from the top of the stands. A bunch of people laughed, but it was a tense laughter. Over by the bench, K.C. bowed his head and heaved for breath as his coach whispered in his ear.

"This sucks," Sage said from a few rows up. "He's undefeated. He can't let this ape man beat him."

The ref blew his whistle and K.C. and Wolverine approached the mat again. Everyone gasped when Wolverine came right at K.C. and flipped him over onto his back. My hands automatically flew to my mouth. Normally the wrestlers circled each other for at least a few seconds, but Wolverine was clearly out for blood. I guess he was gunning to go down in history as the first person to beat K. C. Lawrence, Junior Olympic champion.

"This is ridiculous," Chandra said as K.C. strained and struggled. His teeth bared, his face reddened, the tendons in his neck could have given Coach Holmes' a run for their money. "We have to do something."

"Like what?" Mindy asked.

Daniel suddenly jumped to his feet.

"Let's go, K.C. !" Clap, clap, clapclapclap.

My heart dropped and I looked up at him. I couldn't have been more surprised if Oprah Winfrey had just walked in wearing a crab costume. Was Daniel actually trying to start a chant? "What're you doing?" I asked, breaking into a smile.

He widened his eyes slightly, urging me to join him. Actually, *begging* me to join him.

"Let's go, K.C. !" Clap, clap, clapclapclap.

This time he threw in a punch up, punch out. He was doing arm movements! All alone in the middle of the crowd. Maybe tossing him and his buddies out there for a pep rally on their own really *had* changed something.

But that didn't mean I should leave him hanging again. I stood up and joined in.

"Let's go, K.C. !" we shouted.

Chandra looked up at us and grinned. She pulled Jaimee up and joined in the cheer.

"Let's go, K.C. !" Clap, clap, clapclapclap.

On the next chant a male voice from high up in the bleachers joined us. I turned around and grinned when I saw that it was Terrell. He punched his arm up and shouted at the top of his lungs. Slowly Joe stood up to join him.

"On your feet, everyone!" Chandra cried.

"Let's go, K.C. !" Clap, clap, clapclapclap.

All around us the other cheerleaders joined in. Mindy, Sage, Autumn, Lindsey, Karianna. Down a few rows the new girls, Shira, Wendy and Ally, jumped up. Soon various members of the crowd started chanting as well and the words filled the small gym.

"Let's go, K.C. !" Clap, clap, clapclapclap.

Down on the mat, K.C. let out a guttural growl and suddenly, he shoved Wolverine's shoulders back and flipped him over, their legs a tangled, struggling mess.

"Point! Sand Dune!" the ref shouted.

Everyone in the Sand Dune stands cheered and the chant grew louder.

"Let's go, K.C. !"

I heard a pounding on the bleachers and looked over to find Tara, Phoebe and Whitney rushing down the steps, taking them two at a time. They lined up in front of the stands and shouted up at the crowd, bringing everyone into it.

"Let's go, K.C. !" Clap, clap, clapclapclap.

K.C. and his opponent were standing now and K.C. circled him, on his toes, his arms stretched and ready for attack. The confusion and exhaustion were gone. He looked alert, energized, ready to fight. Suddenly Wolverine came at him and K.C. grabbed him, this time using his momentum against him to flip *him* over.

"Let's go, K.C.!" Clap, clap, clapclapclap.

Tara was grinning. Whitney was bouncing up and down on her toes, maybe riled after a few weeks without cheering. I glanced at Mindy and we smiled. The energy in the room had completely shifted. We had gone from lowest of the low to super positive with one chant. Then Tara pointed up at the stands and laughed. I turned around and saw that her boyfriend, Bobby Goow—the original male-cheerleader tease-meister—had joined in. And he was really into it, clapping with a serious expression like he could personally strengthen K.C. Sweet.

"Let's go, K.C. !" Clap, clap, clapclapclap.

Down on the bench, even Christopher Healy and some of the other wrestlers joined in.

Wolverine was struggling to keep his shoulders off the ground. K.C. grappled and groped, twisting his arms through and around his opponent's until they were pretzeled together in a configuration that hardly looked natural or comfortable. Wolverine grunted and groaned, but it was clear he was struggling against an inevitable death. Finally, K.C. let out a cry that sounded something like a bear's roar, and Wolverine's shoulders hit the ground.

"Pin! Sand Dune! Winner!" the referee shouted.

The crowd went bonkers. Tara, Whitney and Phoebe jumped up and down, screaming. K.C. got up and thrust his fists to the air. Jaimee hugged me from behind, nearly tackling me into the woman in front of me. All around me everyone was laughing and high-fiving and a couple of people even kissed.

Down on the bench, Christopher Healy turned around and pointed at Daniel. He knew his brother had been instrumental in that win. Guess he wouldn't be teasing my man anymore.

Daniel grabbed me and suddenly we were hugging and cheering and kissing. I couldn't have been more proud of him. My boyfriend was a true cheerleader.

• • •

"That was awesome!" Terrell shouted, his breath making steam clouds in the cold air. "That was freakin' awesome!"

Dozens of people had gathered together outside the school to wait for K.C.'s emergence from the locker room. Everyone around us laughed at Terrell's antics. He was like a manic kindergartner on too much Kool-Aid, unable to sit still for even two seconds. He kept pacing around, bending at the waist as he hooted and hollered. Boy was fired *up*.

"What do you think's gonna happen when he comes down?" Chandra whispered to me.

"I don't know, but I hope he's not operating any heavy machinery when it happens," I said.

The doors to the school opened and K.C. walked out, his long hair slicked back into a ponytail and his face still ruddy from the exertion of the match. The entire crowd cheered his arrival and K.C. ducked his head sheepishly. He loped right over to Daniel and offered his hand, which Daniel happily slapped, then pulled K.C. into a hug. Terrell rushed over and clapped K.C. on the back, bouncing up and down.

"That was an incredible comeback, man," Daniel said.

"Couldn't have done it without you guys," K.C. replied.

Terrell blew out a scoff. "Please."

"No, man. I'm serious," K.C. said. "I was totally lost out there, but when you guys started cheering for me . . . I don't know . . . I just got this burst of energy. It was so cool. I totally fed off the crowd."

Daniel and Terrell both grinned, flushed with pleasure.

"So thanks, all of you," K.C. said, addressing the crowd. "I guess this was a group victory."

"Whoo-hoo!" Chandra cheered, and everyone laughed.

The crowd started to break up as some of the fans went over to congratulate K.C. Gradually the cheerleading squad came together in the mayhem. Everyone in our circle was smiling, but there was still this uncertainty in the air. What, if anything, had changed?

"Think things will go back to normal again now?" Jaimee asked.

"Define normal," Tara replied.

She had a point. Nothing had been normal since the guys

231

had crashed our squad. We still had to *find* normal. For a long moment, no one said anything. Inside, I started to panic. Maybe nothing *had* changed.

"So, how does it feel?" Tara said finally.

"How does what feel?" Terrell asked.

"How does it feel to change the outcome of a match?" Tara asked.

The guys exchanged long looks. They shifted their feet. And slowly, they started to smile.

"It feels pretty unbelievable," Daniel said finally.

Laughter trickled throughout the squad. Relieved, happy laughter.

"I didn't really know that was possible," Steven said. "You guys are really an integral part of the team."

"*We* are?" I asked pointedly.

"We *all* are," Daniel amended, looking right at me, his blue eyes intense.

Spin city. My heart, my head, my everything spun.

"Look, we want you all to know we're gonna take things more seriously from now on," Terrell said. He cleared his throat, swallowing his pride, maybe. "No more crap."

"So . . . you'll respect the props box?" Autumn asked.

"Yep."

"And you'll actually do work at craft nights?" Jaimee asked.

"Yep."

"And you'll do whatever fundraisers *we* want to do?" Tara asked.

"Now those I think we should vote on," Terrell said, lifting a finger.

We all muttered our agreement. After all, Daniel had

turned out to be a marketing genius. Maybe he had a few more tricks up his sleeve.

"All right, all right," Tara said, raising her hands. "We'll vote on the fundraisers."

"And you'll invite us to your next slumber party?" Steven asked.

"Uh, no," Tara said. "But maybe we'll figure out an activity we can all go to together."

"Toga?" Daniel suggested.

"Strip poker?" Joe put in.

Chandra narrowed her eyes. "You dudes better quit while you're ahead."

Daniel glanced at the fan buses, which were already packed with people and waiting for us by the curb.

"How about we start with Dolly's?" he suggested, slipping his hand into mine. "We all have our cars back at the school. We can caravan from there."

"Sounds like a plan to me," I said. "Everybody in?"

And for once, we all agreed on something.

On Monday morning we all arrived at school early and were gathered outside the door to the main office. I had even dressed up for the occasion, wearing a black skirt and the light blue V-neck sweater my mother had given me for Christmas. Apparently everyone else had had the same idea. The guys wore button-downs and pants instead of jeans and sweats and the girls had all cleaned up quite nicely.

"Now remember, Terrell and I are going to do the talking, all right?" Tara whispered, her hand on the doorknob.

Everyone nodded. I felt like we were a bunch of little kids looking up at our kindergarten teacher in awe. I couldn't believe Tara and Terrell had the guts to do this. But when it came to bravery in the face of authority figures, those two had more than cornered the market.

"Okay, here goes nothing," Terrell said. Tara pushed open the door and we all followed our two fearless leaders into the office.

Betty, the head secretary, looked up from her computer in surprise. Behind her, the phones rang off the hook and her two assistants scurried around, jotting down the names of the kids that were being called in sick and checking the attendance records.

"What's all this?" Betty asked.

"We'd like to talk to Principal Bu—" Tara began, then bit her tongue.

I glanced at Chandra and tried not to laugh. Buzzkill was not, in fact, his real name.

"We'd like to talk to the principal," Terrell said helpfully.

Betty looked intrigued. I bet no one loved a good piece of gossip better than the school secretaries. They knew everything that went on around this place.

"And what is this regarding?" she asked, reaching for her intercom button.

"An apology," Tara said, clearing her throat.

Betty frowned and hit the button. "Sir? The cheerleading squad is here to see you."

There was a moment of relative silence as the intercom hummed. "The whole squad?"

Betty hoisted herself out of her chair to see better over the high counter and counted us up quickly, her lips moving as she went. "Yes, sir," she said.

"Send them in."

"Go right ahead," Betty said.

Tara strode over, head held high, and opened the door. Principal Buzzkill was just standing up and fastening the button on his suit jacket as she did so.

"Well, come right in, Miss Timothy," he said.

We all crowded into the tiny office together, sardining ourselves in shoulder to shoulder in order to fit. Principal Buzzkill just barely hid a smile of amusement at our discomfort. He cleared his throat and arranged his features into a frown.

"We're sorry, sir," Terrell said respectfully, at the head of the crowd with Tara. "We're just a little bit excited."

I glanced at Daniel, impressed.

"Kid's good," he whispered with a shrug. Then he lifted his arm to put it behind me and give us both more room. Surreptitiously he placed his hand on my back and I smiled.

"Excited?" The principal was nonplussed. "I'd think you'd be more chagrined, considering we've finally decided upon your punishment for last week's debacle."

Oh, God. We were too late.

"We're here to ask you to forgo that punishment," Tara chimed in.

His eyebrows shot up. "Are you?"

"Yes. We are. We know what we did was wrong and we're here to ask you for a chance to make it up to you," Tara said.

"And to the school," Terrell added.

The principal looked us all over as if trying to decide whether this was some kind of practical joke. Not that I could blame him. We were, after all, renowned for that kind of thing.

"And how do you propose to do that?" he asked finally.

"We want to hold another pep rally," Tara told him. "This Friday."

"We think it would be good to erase the memory of the last one as quickly as possible," Terrell added.

"And you really think you can do that," Principal Buzz-kill said.

"If we put together a really kickass—" Terrell stopped under a stern look from the principal and shifted his feet. "I mean, a really *awesome* program," he amended. "Sir."

The principal took a deep breath and looked at the ceiling. "So . . . let me get this straight. You want me to not punish you and instead you want me to let you throw another pep rally, even though you completely ruined the last one. You want me to let eight hundred students out of class early, *again,* and just trust that you won't mess it up."

Well, when you put it that way . . .

"Yes, sir. We do," Tara said.

"And why should I do that?" he asked.

"Because we're really sorry," Jaimee piped in.

"And we love this school," Phoebe added.

"And we won't let you down again . . . sir," Daniel said.

"If we do, you can give us four weeks of detention and make us clean all the bathrooms," I announced.

There was a collective gasp in the room and everyone turned to glare at me. Oops.

"That's the first sane idea I've heard all morning," Principal Buzzkill said with a smile. "Annisa Gobrowski, you have a deal. You all can throw your pep rally, but if any of you is late, if any of you shows up without your uniform, if any of you has so much as one iota of attitude, you're all in detention for four weeks."

Oh man. Oh man, oh man, oh man.

"But I can't make you clean the bathrooms," he said. "I'll have a union situation on my hands."

We all stood there uncertainly as he sniffed and sat back down in his leather chair, unbuttoning his jacket once again. "You're dismissed," he said.

Slowly everyone turned and filed out. A half dozen hands smacked various parts of my body. My arms, my back, the back of my head.

"Well, what?" I said as we emerged into the hall. "We're not gonna let him down, are we? I mean, that was the whole plan."

"She has a point," Chandra said.

"Thank you!" I replied, rubbing my arm where someone's fingernail had left a mark. Daniel put his arm around my shoulder and kissed the top of my head. I leaned gratefully into his side.

"She does have a point," Tara said with a nod. "Yeah. This is going to be the most kicka—I mean *awesome* pep rally ever!" she said, earning laughter all around. "All right. Hands in."

We all did as we were told, right there in the center of the hallway, as students and teachers started to make their way to their classrooms and lockers all around us.

"On three," Tara said. "One, two, three."

"Whaddup, Sand *Dune*!"

We all threw our hands into the air and didn't even care that everyone in the hallway was staring. The squad had officially jelled. And we were ready to kick a little *awesome*.

• • •

"Fighting Crabs up in the stands, let's—hear you—shout! Fighting Crabs up in the stands, let's—hear you—now! All you fans, yell 'Go!' "

"GO!"

Daniel and I executed a perfect chair sit as the entire student body shouted back at us. We cradled out and I grinned up at him before my feet hit the floor. This was working. This was working *well*. Not only was everyone psyched up for a pep rally that actually had spirit, but all day kids I didn't even know had been coming up and thanking me for helping them get out of class once again. Bethany had actually fallen on her knees and kissed my feet when she heard. It was a win-win situation, really.

"All you fans, yell 'Crabs!'"

"CRABS!"

Coach Holmes beamed at us from the bleachers. Even better, Coach Rincon was sitting next to her, their thighs touching. Daniel and Terrell had called him and begged him to come, saying he shouldn't let us come between him and the love of his life. Coach Rincon had agreed, and right before the pep rally, he and Coach Holmes had had a long talk (apparently, like Daniel and me, lack of communication had been *their* problem as well), then kissed and made up. Not that I was spying or anything. Really.

This time Tara and Phoebe had done the dirty work and reported back.

As I went up in a double-base extension, Coach Rincon looked like a proud papa. Tara handed me the "Crabs" sign from the floor and I clutched it in both hands.

"GO!" we all shouted as Phoebe thrust her sign in the air.

"CRABS!"

I held my sign up above my head and saw Bethany snap a picture from the center of the crowd. Below me the guys' arms were solid as rocks. They should have been after a week's worth of extra practices and weight-room time. All week long everyone had rallied, staying even later after school to work out and coming in early to make signs and banners. Now it was finally paying off.

"GO!"

The crowd was so loud, there was going to be an outbreak of laryngitis.

"CRABS!"

I seriously thought I saw someone's voice box pop out.

"GO!"

"CRABS!"

"LET'S GO, CRABS!"

The crowd went wild and I tossed the sign to the floor. There were Mindy and Whitney and Erin, cheering along with the rest of the girls' basketball team. There was K.C., spinning a rally towel in the air at the tip-top of the bleachers, shouting at the top of his lungs. Even Christopher, Bobby and their friends were cheering. If that wasn't a successful pep rally, I don't know what was.

I cradled out, kissed Daniel in glee and thrust my hands into the air. In the corner of the gym, Principal Buzzkill applauded with the rest of the faculty. As we all looked, he flashed us a thumbs-up. No detention. No punishment. Nothing but bikini car washes and coed sleepovers from here on out.

Just kidding.

But one thing was totally clear as we all hugged and ran off the court: the pride. Everyone from Tara to Phoebe to Joe to Steven was beaming with the stuff. After all, the All-New (and Improved) Sand Dune High School Fighting Crabs cheerleaders had finally come together to save ourselves and our season. That was something that any cheerleader, whether from Mars *or* from Venus, could be proud of.

KIERAN SCOTT was a non-blonde cheerleader in high school (though she experimented with Sun-In often and with psychedelic results). A graduate of Rutgers University, Kieran grew up in Montvale, New Jersey, and now lives with her husband, Matt, in Westwood, just a few towns away. She is currently working hard on her next novel.